TALES *of* FAIRIES, WITCHES *and* MAGIC

Gayatri Kalra Sehgal is an internationally acclaimed author, an artist and a passionate educationist. She set up a daycare centre and two schools, first as the principal and later as a dean, and carefully designed their academic curricula. In 2013, she innovated and revolutionized a novel way of writing report cards, renaming them as 'Child's Intelligence Profile'.

She regularly conducts interactive seminars and engaging workshops on the National Education Policy 2020 (NEP 2020), child development, learning styles, curriculum design, effective communication, authorpreneurship, emotional well-being during the pandemic, and more, sensitizing educators towards holistic teaching and learning approaches. Her work, including her motivational speeches, is aimed at encouraging awareness and sensitivity, and offering support to parents of differently-abled children.

Her 13 published books are an extensive collection of her unique experiences and her vision to inspire global leaders for tomorrow.

Also by the Author

Greatest Ever Aesop's Fables

Stories of Dragons and Beasts

Become a Mathematician in 21 Days

Become a Brilliant Thinker in 21 Days

Become a Creative Genius in 21 Days

Being a Mathematician: Mastering Secrets of Mental Math

Being a Brilliant Thinker: Mastering Intelligent Thinking Skills

Being a Creative Genius: Mastering Activities That Inspire Creativity

Super Child! Unlocking the Secrets of Working Memory

Winning Strategies for Parents: Helping Your Child Excel at Home and School

TALES *of* FAIRIES, WITCHES *and* MAGIC

Gayatri Kalra Sehgal

RUPA

Published by
Rupa Publications India Pvt. Ltd 2023
7/16, Ansari Road, Daryaganj
New Delhi 110002

Sales centres:
Bengaluru Chennai
Hyderabad Jaipur Kathmandu
Kolkata Mumbai Prayagraj

P-ISBN: 978-93-5702-840-0
E-ISBN: 978-93-5702-758-8

First impression 2023

10 9 8 7 6 5 4 3 2 1

Printed in India

To my sons,
Divyamshu and Kuber

Contents

1

Cinderella

Once upon a time there was a gentleman who took for a second wife the haughtiest and proudest woman that had ever been seen. She had two daughters of the same temper, and who resembled her in everything. The husband, on his side, had a daughter, but whose gentleness and goodness were without parallel. She inherited them from her mother, who was the best creature in the world.

The wedding was hardly over before the stepmother's ill-humour broke out. She could not abide the young girl, whose good qualities made her own daughters appear more detestable. She employed her in all the meanest work of the house. It was she who cleaned the plate, and the stairs, who scrubbed Madame's chamber, and those of Mesdemoiselles, her daughters.

She slept at the top of the house, in a loft, on a wretched straw mattress, while her sisters occupied rooms, beautifully floored, in which were the most fashionable beds, and mirrors wherein they could see themselves from head to foot.

The poor girl bore everything with patience, and did not dare complain to her father, who would only have scolded her, as his wife governed him entirely. When she had done her work, she went and placed herself in the chimney-corner, and sat down amongst the cinders, which caused her to be called by the household in general Cindertail.

The second daughter, however, who was not so rude as her elder sister, called her Cinderella. Notwithstanding, Cinderella, in her shabby clothes, looked a thousand times handsomer than her sisters, however magnificently attired.

It happened that the King's son gave a ball, and invited to it all persons of quality. Our two young ladies were included in the invitation, for they cut a great figure in the neighbourhood. Behold them in great delight, and very busy choosing the most becoming gowns and head-dresses. A new mortification for Cinderella, for it was she who ironed her sisters' linen, and set their ruffles. Nothing was talked of but the style in which they were to be dressed.

'I,' said the eldest, 'will wear my red velvet dress and my English point-lace trimmings.'

'I,' said the youngest, 'shall only wear my usual petticoat; but to make up for that, I shall put on my gold-flowered mantua, and my necklace of diamonds, which are none of the poorest.'

They sent for a good milliner to make up their double-frilled caps, and bought their patches of the best maker. They called Cinderella to give them her opinion, for she had excellent taste. Cinderella gave them the best advice in the world, and even offered to dress their heads for them, which they were very willing she should do; and whilst she was about it, they said to her, 'Cinderella, shouldst thou like to go to the ball?'

'Alas! Mesdemoiselles, you make game of me; that would not befit me at all.'

'Thou art right, they would laugh immensely to see a Cindertail at a ball!'

Any other but Cinderella would have dressed their heads awry, but she was good natured, and dressed them to perfection. They could eat nothing for nearly two days, so transported were they with joy. More than a dozen laces were broken in making their waists as small as possible, and they were always before their looking-glasses.

At last the happy day arrived. They set off, and Cinderella followed them with her eyes as long as she could. When they were out of sight, she began to cry. Her fairy godmother, who saw her all in tears, inquired what ailed her.

'I should so like—I should so like—' she sobbed so much that she could not finish the sentence.

'Thou wouldst so like to go to the ball—is not that it?'

'Alas! yes,' said Cinderella, sighing.

'Well, if thou wilt be a good girl, I will take care thou shalt go.' She led her into her chamber, and said to her, 'Go into the garden and bring me a pumpkin.'

Cinderella went immediately, gathered the finest she could find, and brought it to her godmother, unable to guess how the pumpkin could enable her to go to the ball. Her godmother scooped it out; and, having left nothing but the rind, struck it with her wand, and the pumpkin was immediately changed into a beautiful coach gilt all over.

She then went and looked into the mouse-trap, where she found six mice, all alive. She told Cinderella to lift the door of the mouse-trap a little, and to each mouse, as it ran out, she gave a tap with her wand, and the mouse was immediately changed into a fine horse, thereby producing a handsome team of six horses, of a beautiful dappled mouse-grey colour.

As she was in some difficulty as to what she should make a coachman of, Cinderella said, 'I will go and see if there be not a rat in the rat-trap; we will make a coachman of him.'

'Thou art right,' said her godmother. 'Go and see.'

Cinderella brought her the rat-trap, in which there were three great rats. The godmother selected one from the three, on account of its ample beard, and having touched it, it was changed into a fat coachman, who had the finest moustaches that ever were seen.

She then said, 'Go into the garden, thou wilt find there, behind the watering-pot, six lizards, bring them to me.'

She had no sooner brought them than the godmother transformed them into six footmen, who immediately jumped up behind the coach, with their liveries all covered with lace, and hung on to it as if they had done nothing else all their lives.

The fairy godmother then said to Cinderella, 'Well, there is something to go to the ball in. Art thou not well pleased?'

'Yes, but am I to go in these dirty clothes?'

Her godmother only touched her with her wand, and in the same instant her dress was changed to cloth of gold and silver, covered with jewels. She then gave her a pair of glass slippers, the prettiest in the world.

When she was thus attired, she got into the coach; but her godmother advised her, above all things, not to stay out past midnight—warning her, that if she remained at the ball one minute longer, her coach would again become a pumpkin; her horses, mice; her footmen, lizards; and her clothes resume their old appearance. She promised her godmother she would not fail to leave the ball before midnight, and departed, out of her senses with joy.

The King's son, who was informed that a grand Princess had arrived whom nobody knew, ran to receive her. He handed her out of the coach and led her into the hall, where the company was assembled. There was immediately a dead silence; they stopped dancing, and the fiddlers ceased to play, so engrossed was every one in the contemplation of the great attractions of the unknown lady. Nothing was heard but a low murmur of 'Oh! how lovely she is!' The King himself, old as he was, could not take his eyes from her, and observed to the Queen, that it was a long time since he had seen so beautiful and so amiable a person. All the ladies were intently occupied in examining her head-dress and her clothes, that they might have some like them the very next day, provided they could find materials as beautiful, and work people sufficiently clever to make them up.

The King's son conducted her to the most honourable seat, and then led her out to dance. She danced with so much grace that their admiration of her was increased. A very grand supper was served, of which the Prince ate not a morsel, so absorbed was he in contemplation of her. She seated herself beside her sisters, and showed them a thousand civilities. She shared with them the oranges and citrons which the Prince had given to her; at which they were much surprised, for she appeared a perfect stranger to them.

Whilst they were in conversation together, Cinderella heard the clock strike three-quarters past eleven. She immediately made a profound curtsey to the company, and departed as quickly as she could.

As soon as she had reached home, she went to find her godmother; and after having thanked her, said she much wished to go to the ball again the next day, because the King's son had invited her.

While she was occupied in telling her godmother all that had passed at the ball, the two sisters knocked at the door. Cinderella went and opened it—'How late you are!' said she to them, yawning, rubbing her eyes, and stretching herself as if she had but just awoke. She had not, however, been inclined to sleep since she had left them.

'Hadst thou been at the ball,' said one of her sisters to

her, 'thou wouldst not have been weary of it. There came to it the most beautiful Princess—the most beautiful that ever was seen. She paid us a thousand attentions. She gave us oranges and citrons.'

Cinderella was beside herself with delight. She asked them the name of the Princess; but they replied that nobody knew her; that the King's son was much puzzled about it, and that he would give everything in the world to know who she was. Cinderella smiled and said, 'She was very handsome, then? Heavens! how fortunate you are!—Could not I get a sight of her? Alas! Mademoiselle Javotte, lend me the yellow gown you wear every day?'

'Truly,' said Mademoiselle Javotte, 'I like that! Lend one's gown to a dirty Cindertail like you!—I must be very mad indeed!'

Cinderella fully expected this refusal, and was delighted at it, for she would have been greatly embarrassed if her sister had lent her her gown.

The next day the two sisters went to the ball, and Cinderella also, but still more splendidly dressed than before. The King's son never left her side, or ceased saying tender things to her. The young lady was much amused, and forgot what her godmother had advised her, so that she heard the clock begin to strike twelve when she did not even think it was eleven.

She rose and fled as lightly as a fawn. The Prince followed her, but could not overtake her. She dropped one of her glass slippers, which the Prince carefully picked up.

Cinderella reached home almost breathless, without coach or footmen, and in her shabby clothes, nothing having remained of all her finery, except one of her little slippers, the fellow of that she had let fall. The guards at the palace gate were asked if they had not seen a Princess go out; they answered that they had seen no one pass but a poorly-dressed girl, who had more the air of a peasant than of a lady.

When the two sisters returned from the ball, Cinderella asked them if they had been as much entertained as before, and if the beautiful lady had been present. They said yes, but that she had fled as soon as it had struck twelve, and so precipitately that she had let fall one of her little glass slippers, the prettiest in the world; that the King's son had picked it up; that he had done nothing but gaze upon it during the remainder of the evening; and that, undoubtedly, he was very much in love with the beautiful person to whom the little slipper belonged.

They spoke the truth; for a few days afterwards the King's son caused it to be proclaimed by sound of trumpet that he would marry her whose foot would exactly match with the slipper. They began by trying it on the Princesses, then on the Duchesses, and so on throughout all the Court; but in vain. It was taken to the two sisters, who did their utmost to force one of their feet into the slipper, but they could not manage to do so.

Cinderella, who witnessed their efforts and recognised the slipper, said, laughingly, 'Let me see if it will not fit me.'

Her sisters began to laugh and ridicule her. The gentleman

who had been entrusted to try the slipper, having attentively looked at Cinderella and found her to be very handsome, said that it was a very proper request, and that he had been ordered to try the slipper on all girls without exception. He made Cinderella sit down, and putting the slipper to her little foot, he saw it go on easily and fit like wax.

Great was the astonishment of the two sisters, but it was still greater when Cinderella took the other little slipper out of her pocket and put it on her other foot.

At that moment the fairy godmother arrived, who having given a tap with her wand to Cinderella's clothes, they became still more magnificent than all the others she had appeared in. The two sisters then recognised in her the beautiful person they had seen at the ball. They threw themselves at her feet to crave her forgiveness for all the ill-treatment she had suffered from them. Cinderella raised and embracing them, said that she forgave them with all her heart, and begged them to love her dearly for the future. They conducted her to the young Prince, dressed just as she was.

He found her handsomer than ever, and a few days afterwards he married her. Cinderella, who was as kind as she was beautiful, gave her sisters apartments in the palace, and married them the very same day to two great lords of the court.

Beauty in woman is a treasure rare
Which we are never weary of admiring;
But a sweet temper is a gift more fair
And better worth the youthful maid's desiring.

That was the boon bestowed on Cinderella
By her wise godmother—her truest glory.
The rest was 'nought but leather and prunella.'
Such is the moral of this little story—

Beauties, that charm becomes you more than dress,
And wins a heart with far greater facility.
In short, in all things to ensure success,
The real fairy gift is Amiability!

Also,

Talent, courage, wit, and worth
Are rare gifts to own on earth.

But if you want to thrive at court—
So, at least, the wise report—
You will find you need some others,
Such as god-fathers or mothers.

2

Riquet with the Tuft

Once upon a time there was a Queen, who was brought to bed of a son so ugly and so ill-shaped that it was for a long time doubtful if he possessed a human form. A Fairy, who was present at his birth, affirmed that he would not fail to be amiable, as he would have much good-sense. She added, even, that he would be able, in consequence of the gift she had endowed him with, to impart equal intelligence to the person he should love best. All this consoled the poor Queen a little, who was much distressed at having brought into the world so hideous a little monkey.

It is true that the child was no sooner able to speak than he said a thousand pretty things, and that there was in all his actions an indescribable air of intelligence which charmed one.

I had forgotten to say that he was born with a little tuft of hair on his head, which occasioned him to be named Riquet with the Tuft; for Riquet was the family name.

At the end of seven or eight years, the Queen of a neighbouring kingdom was brought to bed of two daughters. The first that came into the world was fairer than day. The Queen was so delighted, that it was feared her great joy would prove hurtful to her.

The same Fairy who had assisted at the birth of little Riquet with the Tuft was present upon this occasion, and to moderate the joy of the Queen, she declared to her that this little Princess would have no mental capacity, and that she would be as stupid as she was beautiful.

This mortified the Queen exceedingly; but a few minutes afterwards she experienced a very much greater annoyance, for the second girl she gave birth to, proved to be extremely ugly.

'Do not distress yourself so much, Madam,' said the Fairy to her. 'Your daughter will find compensation; she will have so much sense that her lack of beauty will scarcely be perceived.'

'Heaven send it may be so,' replied the Queen; 'but are there no means of giving a little sense to the eldest, who is so lovely?'

'I can do nothing for her, Madam, in the way of wit,' said the Fairy, 'but everything in that of beauty; and as there is nothing in my power that I would not do to gratify you, I will endow her with the ability to render beautiful the person who shall please her.'

As these two Princesses grew up, their endowments

increased in the same proportion, and nothing was talked of anywhere but the beauty of the eldest and the intelligence of the youngest. It is true that their defects also greatly increased with their years. The youngest became uglier every instant, and the eldest more stupid every day. She either made no answer when she was spoken to, or she said something foolish. With this she was so awkward, that she could not place four pieces of china on a mantel-shelf without breaking one of them, nor drink a glass of water without spilling half of it on her dress.

Notwithstanding the great advantage of beauty to a girl, the youngest bore away the palm from her sister nearly always, in every society. At first they gathered round the handsomest, to gaze at and admire her; but they soon left her for the wittiest, to listen to a thousand agreeable things; and people were astonished to find that, in less than a quarter of an hour, the eldest had not a soul near her, and that all the company had formed a circle round the youngest.

The former, though very stupid, noticed this, and would have given, without regret, all her beauty for half the sense of her sister. The Queen, discreet as she was, could not help reproaching her frequently with her folly, which made the poor Princess ready to die of grief.

One day that she had withdrawn into a wood to bewail her misfortune, she saw a little man approach her, of most disagreeable appearance, but dressed very magnificently. It was the young Prince Riquet with the Tuft, who, having fallen in love with her from seeing her portraits, which were sent all round the world, had quitted his father's kingdom to have the pleasure of beholding and speaking to her. Enchanted to meet her thus alone, he accosted her with all the respect and politeness imaginable. Having remarked, after paying the usual compliments, that she was very melancholy, he said to her, 'I cannot comprehend, Madam, how a person so beautiful as you are can be so sad as you appear; for though I may boast of having seen an infinity of lovely women, I can avouch that I have never beheld one whose beauty could be compared to yours.'

'You are pleased to say so, Sir,' replied the Princess; and there she stopped.

'Beauty,' continued Riquet, 'is so great an advantage, that it ought to surpass all others; and when one possesses it, I do not see anything that could very much distress you.'

'I had rather,' said the Princess, 'be as ugly as you, and have good sense, than possess the beauty I do, and be as stupid as I am.'

'There is no greater proof of good sense, Madam, than the belief that we have it not; it is the nature of that gift, that the more we have, the more we believe we are deficient of it.'

'I do not know how that may be,' said the Princess, 'but I know well enough that I am very stupid, and that is the cause of the grief which is killing me.'

'If that is all that afflicts you, Madam, I can easily put an end to your sorrow.'

'And how would you do that?' said the Princess.

'I have the power, Madam,' said Riquet with the Tuft,

'to give as much wit as any one can possess to the person I love the most; and as you, Madam, are that person, it will depend entirely upon yourself whether or not you will have so much wit, provided that you are willing to marry me.'

The Princess was thunderstruck, and replied not a word. 'I see,' said Riquet with the Tuft, 'that this proposal pains you; and I am not surprised at it; but I give you a full year to consider of it.'

The Princess had so little sense, and at the same time was so anxious to have a great deal, that she thought the end of that year would never come; so she accepted at once the offer that was made her.

She had no sooner promised Riquet with the Tuft that she would marry him that day twelve months later, than she felt herself to be quite another person to what she was previously. She found she possessed an incredible facility of saying anything she wished, and of saying it in a shrewd, yet easy and natural manner. She commenced on the instant, and kept up a sprightly conversation with Riquet with the Tuft, during which she chatted away at such a rate, that Riquet with the Tuft began to believe he had given her more wit than he had kept for himself.

When she returned to the Palace, the whole Court was puzzled to account for a change so sudden and extraordinary, for in proportion to the number of foolish things they had heard her say formerly, were the sensible and exceedingly clever observations she now gave utterance to. All the Court was in a state of joy which is not to be conceived.

The younger sister alone was not very much pleased, as no longer possessing over her elder sister the advantage of wit, she now only appeared, by her side, as a very disagreeable-looking person.

The King was now led by his eldest daughter's advice, and sometimes even held his Council in her apartment. The news of this alteration having spread abroad, all the young Princes of the neighbouring kingdoms exerted themselves to obtain her affection, and nearly all of them asked her hand in marriage; but she found none of them sufficiently intelligent, and she listened to all of them without engaging herself to any one.

At length arrived a Prince so rich, so witty, and so handsome, that she could not help feeling an inclination for him. Her father, having perceived it, told her that he left her at perfect liberty to choose a husband for herself, and that she had only to make known her decision. As the more sense we possess, the more difficulty we find in making up one's mind positively on such a matter, she requested, after having thanked her father, that he would allow her some time to think of it. She went, by chance, to walk in the same wood where she had met with Riquet with the Tuft, in order to ponder with greater freedom on what she had to do.

While she was walking, deep in thought, she heard a dull sound beneath her feet, as of many persons running to and fro, and busily occupied. Having listened more attentively, she heard one say, 'Bring me that saucepan;' another, 'Give me that kettle;' another, 'Put some wood on the fire.' At the same moment the ground opened, and she saw beneath her what appeared to be a large kitchen, full of cooks, scullions, and all sorts of servants necessary for the preparation of a magnificent banquet. There came forth a band of twenty to thirty cooks, who went and established themselves in an avenue of the wood at a very long table, and who, each with larding-pin in hand and *the queue de renard* behind the ear, set to work, keeping time to a melodious song.

The Princess, astonished at this sight, inquired for whom they were working. 'Madam,' replied the most prominent of the troop, 'for Prince Riquet with the Tuft, whose marriage will take place to-morrow.' The Princess, still more surprised than she was before, and suddenly recollecting that it was just a twelvemonth from the day on which she had promised to marry Prince Riquet with the Tuft, was lost in amazement.

The cause of her not having remembered her promise was, that when she made it she was a fool, and on receiving her new mind, she forgot all her follies. She had not taken thirty steps in continuation of her walk, when Riquet with the Tuft presented himself before her, gaily and magnificently attired, like a Prince about to be married.

'You see, Madam,' said he, 'I keep my word punctually, and I doubt not but that you have come hither to keep yours, and to make me, by the gift of your hand, the happiest of men.'

'I confess to you, frankly,' replied the Princess, 'that I have not yet made up my mind on that matter, and that I do not think I shall ever be able to do so to your satisfaction.'

'You astonish me, Madam,' said Riquet with the Tuft. 'I have no doubt I do,' said the Princess; 'and assuredly, had I to deal with a stupid person—a man without mind—I should feel greatly embarrassed.'

'A Princess is bound by her word,' he would say to me, 'and you must marry me, as you have promised to do so.'

'But as the person to whom I speak is the most sensible man in all the world, I am certain he will listen to reason. You know that, when I was no better than a fool, I nevertheless could not resolve to marry you—how can you expect, now that I have the sense which you have given me, and which renders me much more difficult to please than before, that I should take a resolution to-day which I could not do then? If you seriously thought of marrying me, you did very wrong to take away my stupidity, and enable me to see clearer than I saw then.'

'If a man without sense,' replied Riquet with the Tuft, 'should meet with some indulgence, as you have just intimated, had he to reproach you with your breach of promise, why would you, Madam, that I should not be equally so in a matter which affects the entire happiness of my life? Is it reasonable that persons of intellect should be in a worse condition than those that have none? Can you assert this—you who have so much and have so earnestly desired to possess it? But let us come to the point, if you please. With the exception of my ugliness, is there anything in me that displeases you? Are you dissatisfied with my birth, my understanding, my temper, or my manners?'

'Not in the least,' replied the Princess; 'I admire in you everything you have mentioned.'

'If so,' rejoined Riquet with the Tuft, 'I shall be happy, as you have it in your power to make me the most agreeable of men.'

'How can that be done?' said the Princess.

'It can be done,' said Riquet with the Tuft, 'if you love me sufficiently to wish that it should be. And in order, Madam, that you should have no doubt about it, know that the same fairy, who, on the day I was born, endowed me with the power to give understanding to the person I chose, gave you also the power to render handsome the man you should love, and on whom you were desirous to bestow that favour.'

'If such be the fact,' said the Princess, 'I wish, with all my heart, that you should become the handsomest Prince in the world, and I bestow the gift on you to the fullest extent in my power.' The Princess had no sooner pronounced these words, than Riquet with the Tuft appeared to her eyes, of all men in the world, the handsomest, the best made, and most amiable she had ever seen.

There are some who assert that it was not the spell of the Fairy, but love alone that caused this metamorphosis. They say that the Princess, having reflected on the perseverance of her lover—on his prudence, and all the good qualities of his heart and mind, no longer saw the deformity of his body nor the ugliness of his features—that his hunch appeared to her nothing more than the effect of a man shrugging his shoulders, and that instead of observing, as she had done, that he limped horribly, she saw in him no more than a certain lounging air, which charmed her. They say also that his eyes, which squinted, seemed to her only more brilliant from that defect, which passed in her mind for a proof of the intensity of his love, and, in fine, that his great red nose had in it something martial and heroic.

However this may be, the Princess promised on the spot to marry him, provided he obtained the consent of the King, her Father. The King, having learned that his daughter entertained a great regard for Riquet with the Tuft, whom he knew also to be a very clever and wise prince, accepted him with pleasure for a son-in-law. The wedding took place the next morning, as Riquet with the Tuft had foreseen, and, according to the instructions which he had given a long time before.

No beauty, no talent, has power above some indefinite charm discerned only by love.

3

The Fairies

There was once a widow who had two daughters. The elder was so like her mother in temper and face, that to have seen the one was to have seen the other. They were both so disagreeable and proud, that it was impossible to live with them. The younger, who was the exact portrait of her father in her kindly and polite ways, was also as beautiful a girl as one could see. As we are naturally fond of those who resemble us, the mother doted on her elder daughter, while for the younger she had a most violent aversion, and made her take her meals in the kitchen and work hard all day. Among other things that she was obliged to do, this poor child was forced to go twice a day to fetch water from a place a mile or more from the house, and carry back a large jug filled to the brim. As she was standing one day by this spring, a poor woman came up to her, and asked the girl to give her some water to drink.

'Certainly, my good woman,' she replied, and the beautiful girl at once stooped and rinsed out the jug, and then, filling it with water from the clearest part of the spring, she held it up to the woman, continuing to support the jug, that she might drink with greater comfort. Having drunk, the woman said to her, 'You are so beautiful, so good and kind, that I cannot refrain from conferring a gift upon you,' for she was really a fairy, who had taken the form of a poor village woman, in order to see how far the girl's kind-heartedness would go.

'This gift I make you,' continued the fairy, 'that with every word you speak, either a flower or a precious stone will fall from your mouth.'

The girl had no sooner reached home than her mother began scolding her for being back so late. 'I am sorry, mother,' said she, 'to have been out so long,' and as she spoke, there fell from her mouth two roses, two pearls, and two large diamonds. The mother gazed at her in astonishment.

'What do I see!' she exclaimed, 'Pearls and diamonds seem to be dropping from her mouth! How is this, my daughter?'—it was the first time she had called her *daughter*.

The poor child related in all simplicity what had happened, letting fall quantities of diamonds in the course of her narrative.

'I must certainly send my other daughter there,' said the mother. 'Look, Fanchon, see what falls from your sister's mouth when she speaks! Would you not be glad to receive a similar gift? All you have to do, is to go and fetch water from the spring, and if an old woman asks you for some to drink, to give it her nicely and politely.'

'I should like to see myself going to the spring,' answered the rude, cross girl.

'I insist on your going,' rejoined the mother, 'and that at once.'

The elder girl went off, still grumbling; with her she took the handsomest silver bottle she could find in the house.

She had no sooner arrived at the spring, than she saw a lady magnificently dressed walking towards her from the wood, who approached and asked for some water to drink. It was the same fairy who had appeared to the sister, but she had now put on the airs and apparel of a princess, as she wished to see how far this girl's rudeness would go.

'Do you think I came here just to draw water for you?' answered the arrogant and unmannerly girl; 'I have, of course, brought this silver bottle on purpose for madam to drink from! Well, all I have to say is—drink from it if you like.'

'You are scarcely polite,' said the fairy, without losing her temper; 'however, as you are so disobliging, I confer this gift upon you, that with every word you speak, a snake or a toad shall fall from your mouth.'

When her mother caught sight of her, she called out,

'Well, my daughter!'

'Well, my mother!' replied the ill-tempered girl, throwing out as she spoke two vipers and two toads.

'Alack!' cried the mother, 'What do I see? This is her

sister's doing, but I will pay her out for it,' and, so saying, she ran towards the younger girl with intent to beat her. The unhappy girl fled from the house, and went and hid herself in a neighbouring forest.

The King's son, who was returning from hunting, met her, and seeing how beautiful she was, asked her what she was doing there all alone, and why she was crying.

'Alas! sir, my mother has driven me from home.'

The King's son, seeing five or six pearls and as many diamonds, falling from her mouth as she spoke, asked her to explain how this was, and she told him all her tale. The King's son fell in love with her, and thinking that such a gift as she possessed was worth more than any ordinary dower brought by another, he carried her off to his father's palace, and there married her.

As for her sister, she made herself so hated, that her own mother drove her from the house. The miserable girl, having gone about in vain trying to find someone who would take her in, crept away into the corner of a wood, and there died.

Of higher worth are gentle words
Than diamonds or gold,
And even o'er the minds of men
A great power they hold.

It costs some pains to be polite,
And needs some kindly thought,
But soon or late, as here you see,
Reward will come unsought.

4

Rapunzel

There were once a man and a woman who had long in vain wished for a child. At length the woman hoped that God was about to grant her desire. These people

had a little window at the back of their house from which a splendid garden could be seen, which was full of the most beautiful flowers and herbs. It was, however, surrounded by a high wall, and no one dared to go into it because it belonged to an enchantress, who had great power and was dreaded by all the world.

One day the woman was standing by this window and looking down into the garden, when she saw a bed which was planted with the most beautiful rampion (rapunzel), and it looked so fresh and green that she longed for it, and had the greatest desire to eat some.

This desire increased every day, and as she knew that she could not get any of it, she quite pined away, and looked pale and miserable. Then her husband was alarmed, and asked, 'What ails you, dear wife?'

'Ah,' she replied, 'if I can't get some of the rampion which is in the garden behind our house, to eat, I shall die.'

The man, who loved her, thought, 'Sooner than let your wife die, bring her some of the rampion yourself, let it cost you what it will.'

In the twilight, he clambered down over the wall into the garden of the enchantress, hastily clutched a handful of rampion, and took it to his wife. She at once made herself a salad of it, and ate it with much relish. She, however, liked it so much, so very much, that the next day she longed for it three times as much as before. If he was to have any rest, her husband must once more descend into the garden. In the gloom of evening, therefore, he let himself down again; but when he had clambered down the wall he was terribly afraid, for he saw the enchantress standing before him.

'How can you dare,' said she with angry look, 'to descend into my garden and steal my rampion like a thief? You shall suffer for it!'

'Ah,' answered he, 'let mercy take the place of justice. I only made up my mind to do it out of necessity. My wife saw your rampion from the window, and felt such a longing for it that she would have died if she had not got some to eat.'

Then the enchantress allowed her anger to be softened, and said to him,

'If the case be as you say, I will allow you to take away with you as much rampion as you will, only I make one condition, you must give me the child which your wife will bring into the world; it shall be well treated, and I will care for it like a mother.'

The man in his terror consented to everything, and when the little one came to them, the enchantress appeared at once, gave the child the name of Rapunzel, and took it away with her.

Rapunzel grew into the most beautiful child beneath the sun. When she was twelve years old, the enchantress shut her into a tower, which lay in a forest, and had neither stairs nor door, but quite at the top was a little window. When the enchantress wanted to go in, she placed herself beneath the tower, and cried,

'Rapunzel, Rapunzel,
Let down your hair to me.'

Rapunzel had magnificent long hair, fine as spun gold, and when she heard the voice of the enchantress she unfastened her braided tresses, wound them round one of the hooks of the window above, and then the hair fell twenty yards down, and the enchantress climbed up by it.

After a year or two, it came to pass that the King's son rode through the forest and went by the tower. Then he heard a song, which was so charming that he stood still and listened. This was Rapunzel, who in her solitude passed her time in letting her sweet voice resound. The King's son wanted to climb up to her, and looked for the door of the tower, but none was to be found. He rode home, but the singing had so deeply touched his heart, that every day he went out into the forest and listened to it.

Once when he was thus standing behind a tree, he saw that an enchantress came there, and he heard how she cried,

'Rapunzel, Rapunzel,
Let down your hair.'

Then Rapunzel let down the braids of her hair, and the enchantress climbed up to her.

'If that is the ladder by which one mounts, I will for once try my fortune,' said he, and the next day, when it began to grow dark, he went to the tower and cried.

'Rapunzel, Rapunzel,
Let down your hair.'

Immediately the hair fell down, and the King's son climbed up.

At first Rapunzel was terribly frightened when a man such as her eyes had never yet beheld came to her; but the King's son began to talk to her quite like a friend, and told her that his heart had been so stirred that it had let him have no rest, and he had been forced to see her. Then Rapunzel lost her fear, and when he asked her if she would take him for a husband, and she saw that he was young and handsome, she thought,

'He will love me more than old Dame Gothel does;' and she said yes, and laid her hand in his. She said, 'I will willingly go away with you, but I do not know how to get down. Bring with you a skein of silk every time that you come, and I will weave a ladder with it, and when that is ready I will descend, and you will take me on your horse.' They agreed that until that time he should come to her every evening, for the old woman came by day.

The enchantress remarked nothing of this, until once Rapunzel said to her, 'Tell me, Dame Gothel, how it happens that you are so much heavier for me to draw up than the young King's son—he is with me in a moment.'

'Ah! you wicked child,' cried the enchantress, 'what do I hear you say! I thought I had separated you from all the world, and yet you have deceived me!' In her anger she clutched Rapunzel's beautiful tresses, wrapped them twice round her left hand, seized a pair of scissors with the right, and snip, snip, they were cut off, and the lovely braids lay on the ground. And she was so pitiless that she took poor Rapunzel into a desert, where she had to live in great grief and misery.

On the same day, however, that she cast out Rapunzel, the enchantress in the evening fastened the braids of hair which she had cut off to the hook of the window, and when the King's son came and cried,

'Rapunzel, Rapunzel,
Let down your hair,'

she let the hair down. The King's son ascended, but he did not find his dearest Rapunzel above, but the enchantress, who gazed at him with wicked and venomous looks.

'Aha!' she cried mockingly. 'You would fetch your dearest, but the beautiful bird sits no longer singing in the nest; the cat has got it, and will scratch out your eyes as well. Rapunzel is lost to you; you will never see her more.'

The King's son was beside himself with pain, and in his despair he leapt down from the tower. He escaped with his life, but the thorns into which he fell pierced his eyes. Then he wandered quite blind about the forest, ate nothing but roots and berries, and did nothing but lament and weep over the loss of his dearest wife. Thus he roamed about in misery for some years, and at length came to the desert where Rapunzel lived in wretchedness.

He heard a voice, and it seemed so familiar to him that he went towards it, and when he approached, Rapunzel knew him and fell on his neck and wept. Two of her tears wetted his eyes, and they grew clear again, and he could see with them as before.

He led her to his kingdom, where he was joyfully received, and they lived for a long time afterwards, happy and contented.

5

Little Snow White

It was in the middle of winter, when the broad flakes of snow were falling around, that a certain queen sat working at her window, the frame of which was made of fine black ebony; and, as she was looking out upon the snow, she pricked her finger, and three drops of blood fell upon it. Then she gazed thoughtfully down on the red drops which sprinkled the white snow and said, 'Would that my little daughter may be as white as that snow, as red as the blood, and as black as the ebony window-frame!' And so the little girl grew up; her skin was a white as snow, her cheeks as rosy as blood, and her hair as black as ebony; and she was called Snow-White.

But this queen died; and the king soon married another wife, who was very beautiful, but so proud that she could not bear to think that any one could surpass her. She had a magical looking-glass, to which she used to go and gaze upon herself in it, and say—

> 'Tell me, glass, tell me true!
> Of all the ladies in the land,
> Who is fairest? Tell me who?'

And the glass answered, 'Thou, Queen, art fairest in the land'

But Snow-White grew more and more beautiful; and when she was seven years old, she was as bright as the day, and fairer than the queen herself. Then the glass one day answered queen, when she went to consult it as usual—

> 'Thou, Queen, may'st fair and beauteous be,
> But Snow-White is lovelier far than thee?'

When the queen heard this she turned pale with rage and envy, and calling to one of her servants said, 'Take Snow-White away into the wide wood, that I may never see her more.' Then the servant led the little girl away; but his heart melted when she begged him to spare her life, and he said, 'I will not hurt thee, thou pretty child.' So he left her there alone; and though he thought it most likely that the wild beasts would tear her to pieces, he felt as if a great weight were taken off his heart when he had made up his mind not to kill her, but leave her to her fate.

Then poor Snow-White wandered along through the wood in great fear; and the wild beasts roared around, but none did her any harm.

In the evening she came to a little cottage, and went in

there to rest, for her weary feet would carry her no further.

Everything was spruce and neat in the cottage: on the table was spread a white cloth, and there were seven little plates with seven little loaves and seven little glasses with wine in them; and knives and forks laid in order, and by the wall stood seven little beds. Then, as she was exceedingly hungry, she picked a little piece off each loaf, and drank a very little wine out of each glass; and after that she thought she would lie down and rest. So she tried all the little beds; and one was too long, and another was too short, till, at last, the seventh suited her; and there she laid herself down and went to sleep.

Presently in came the masters of the cottage, who were seven little dwarfs that lived among the mountains, and dug and searched about for gold. They lighted up their seven lamps, and saw directly that all was not right.

The first said, 'Who has been sitting on my stool?'

The second, 'Who has been eating off my plate?'

The third, 'Who has been picking at my bread?'

The fourth, 'Who has been meddling with my spoon?'

The fifth, 'Who has been handling my fork?'

The sixth, 'Who has been cutting with my knife?'

The seventh, 'Who has been drinking my wine?'

Then the first looked around and said, 'Who has been lying on my bed?' And the rest came running to him, and every one cried out that somebody had been upon his bed. But the seventh saw Snow-White, and called upon his brethren to come and look at her; and they cried out with wonder and astonishment, and brought their lamps and gazing upon her, they said, 'Good heavens! what a lovely child she is!' And they were delighted to see her, and took care not to waken her; and the seventh dwarf slept an hour with each of the other dwarfs in turn, till the night was gone.

In the morning Snow-White told them all her story, and they pitied her, and said if she would keep all things in order, and cook and wash, and knit and spin for them, she might stay where she was, and they would take good care of her. Then they went out all day long to their work, seeking for gold and silver in the mountains; and Snow-White remained at home; and they warned her, saying, 'The queen will soon find out where you are, so take care and let no one in.'

But the queen, now that she thought Snow-White was dead, believed that she was certainly the handsomest lady in the land; so she went to her glass and said—

'Tell me, glass, tell me true!
Of all the ladies in the land,
Who is fairest? Tell me who?'

And the glass answered—

'Thou, Queen, thou art fairest in all this land;
But over the Hills, in the greenwood shade,
Where the seven dwarfs their dwelling have made,
There Snow-White is hiding; and she
Is lovelier far, O Queen, than thee.'

Then the queen was very much alarmed, for she knew that

the glass always spoke the truth, and she was sure that the servant had betrayed her. And as she could not bear to think that any one lived who was more beautiful than she was, she disguised herself as an old pedlar woman and went her way over the hills to the place where the dwarfs dwelt. Then she knocked at the door and cried, 'Fine wares to sell!'

Snow-White looked out of the window, and said, 'Good day, good woman; what have you to sell?'

'Good wares, fine wares,' replied she; 'laces and bobbins of all colours.'

'I will let the old lady in; she seems to be a very good sort of a body,' thought Snow-White; so she ran down, and unbolted the door.

'Bless me!' said the woman, 'how badly your stays are laced. Let me lace them up with one of my nice new laces.'

Snow-White did not dream of any mischief, so she stood up before the old woman who set to work so nimbly, and pulled the lace so tightly that Snow-White lost her breath, and fell down as if she were dead. 'There's an end of all thy beauty,' said the spiteful queen, and went away home.

In the evening the seven dwarfs returned; and I need not say how grieved they were to see their faithful Snow-White stretched upon the ground motionless, as if she were quite dead. However, they lifted her up, and when they found what was the matter, they cut the lace; and in a little time she began to breathe, and soon came to herself again. Then they said, 'The old woman was the queen; take care another time, and let no one in when we are away.'

When the queen got home, she went to her glass, and spoke to it, but to her surprise it replied in the same words as before.

Then the blood ran cold in her heart with spite and malice to hear that Snow-White still lived; and she dressed herself up again in a disguise, but very different from the one she wore before, and took with her a poisoned comb. When she reached the dwarfs' cottage, she knocked at the door, and cried, 'Fine wares to sell!' but Snow-White said, 'I dare not let any one in.'

Then the queen said, 'Only look at my beautiful combs;' and gave her the poisoned one. And it looked so pretty that the little girl took it up and put it into her hair to try it; but the moment it touched her head the poison was so powerful that she fell down senseless. 'There you may lie,' said the queen, and went her way.

But by good luck the dwarfs returned very early that evening; and when they saw Snow-White lying on the ground, they thought what had happened, and soon found the poisoned comb. And when they took it away, she recovered, and told them all that had passed, and they warned her once more not to open the door to any one.

Meanwhile, the queen went home to her glass, and trembled with rage when she received exactly the same answer as before; and she said, 'Snow-White shall die, if it costs me my life.'

So she went secretly into a chamber, and prepared a poisoned apple: the outside looked very rosy and tempting, but whosoever tasted it was sure to die. Then she dressed herself up as a peasant's wife, and travelled over the hills to the dwarfs' cottage, and knocked at the door; but Snow-White put her head out of the window, and said, 'I dare not let any one in, for the dwarfs have told me not to.'

'Do as you please,' said the old woman, 'but at any rate take this pretty apple; I will make you a present of it.'

'No,' said Snow-White, 'I dare not take it.'

'You silly girl!' answered the other, 'What are you afraid of? Do you think it is poisoned? Come! Do you eat one part, and I will eat the other.'

Now the apple was so prepared that one side was good, though the other side was poisoned. Then Snow-White was very much tempted to taste, for the apple looked exceedingly nice; and when she saw the old woman eat, she could refrain no longer. But she had scarcely put the piece into her mouth when she fell down dead upon the ground.

'This time nothing will save thee,' said the queen; and she went home to her glass, and at last it said—'Thou, Queen, art the fairest of all the fair.' And then her envious heart was glad, and as happy as such a heart could be.

When evening came, and the dwarfs returned home, they found Snow-White lying on the ground; no breath passed her lips, and they were afraid that she was quite dead. They lifted her up, and combed her hair, and washed her face with wine and water; but all was in vain.

So they laid her down upon a bier, and all seven watched and bewailed her three whole days; and then they proposed to bury her; but her cheeks were still rosy, and her face looked just as it did while she was alive; so they said, 'We will never bury her in the cold ground.'

And they made a coffin of glass so that they might still look at her, and wrote her name upon it in golden letters, and that she was a king's daughter. Then the coffin was placed upon the hill, and one of the dwarfs always sat by it and watched. And the birds of the air came, too, and bemoaned Snow-White. First of all came an owl, and then a raven, but at last came a dove.

And thus Snow-White lay for a long, long time, and still only looked as though she were asleep; for she was even now as white as snow, and as red as blood, and as black as ebony.

At last a prince came and called at the dwarfs' house; and he saw Snow-White and read what was written in golden letters. Then he offered the dwarfs money, and earnestly prayed them to let him take her away; but they said, 'We will not part with her for all the gold in the world.' At last, however, they had pity on him, and gave him the coffin.

But the moment he lifted it up to carry it home with him, the piece of apple fell from between her lips, and Snow-White awoke, and exclaimed, 'Where am I!'

And the prince answered, 'Thou art safe with me.' Then he told her all that had happened, and said, 'I love you better than all the world; come with me to my father's palace, and you shall be my wife.'

Snow-White consented, and went home with the prince; and everything was prepared with great pomp and splendour for their wedding.

To the feast was invited, among the rest, Snow-White's old enemy, the queen; and as she was dressing herself in fine, rich clothes, she looked in the glass and said—

> Tell me, glass, tell me true!
> Of all the ladies in the land,
> Who is fairest? tell me who?

And the glass answered—

> Thou, lady, art the loveliest *here*, I ween,
> But lovelier far is the new-made queen.

When she heard this, the queen started with rage; but her envy and curiosity were so great, that she could not help setting out to see the bride. And when she arrived, and saw that it was no other than Snow-White, whom she thought had been dead a long while, she choked with passion, and fell ill and died; but Snow-White and the prince lived and reigned happily over that land, many, many years.

6

Rumpelstiltskin

There was once a poor Miller who had a beautiful daughter, and one day, having to go to speak with the King, he said, in order to make himself appear of consequence, that he had a daughter who could spin straw into gold. The King was very fond of gold, and thought to himself,

'That is an art which would please me very well'; and so he said to the Miller, 'If your daughter is so very clever, bring her to the castle in the morning, and I will put her to the proof.'

As soon as she arrived the King led her into a chamber which was full of straw; and, giving her a wheel and a reel, he said, 'Now set yourself to work, and if you have not spun this straw into gold by an early hour to-morrow, you must die.'

With these words he shut the room door, and left the

maiden alone.

There she sat for a long time, thinking how to save her life; for she understood nothing of the art whereby straw might be spun into gold; and her perplexity increased more and more, till at last she began to weep. All at once the door opened, and in stepped a little Man, who said, 'Good evening, fair maiden; why do you weep so sore?'

'Ah,' she replied, 'I must spin this straw into gold, and I am sure I do not know how.'

The little Man asked, 'What will you give me if I spin it for you?'

'My necklace,' said the maiden.

The Dwarf took it, placed himself in front of the wheel, and *whirr, whirr, whirr,* three times round, and the bobbin was full. Then he set up another, and *whirr, whirr, whirr,* thrice round again, and a second bobbin was full; and so he went all night long, until all the straw was spun, and the bobbins were full of gold.

At sunrise the King came, very much astonished to see the gold; the sight of which gladdened him, but did not make his heart less covetous.

He caused the maiden to be led into another room, still larger, full of straw; and then he bade her spin it into gold during the night if she valued her life.

The maiden was again quite at a loss what to do; but while she cried the door opened suddenly, as before, and the Dwarf appeared and asked her what she would give him in return for his assistance.

'The ring off my finger,' she replied. The little Man took the ring and began to spin at once, and by morning all the straw was changed to glistening gold.

The King was rejoiced above measure at the sight of this, but still he was not satisfied, but, leading the maiden into another still larger room, full of straw as the others, he said, 'This you must spin during the night; but if you accomplish it you shall be my bride.'

'For,' thought he to himself, 'a richer wife thou canst not have in all the world.' When the maiden was left alone, the Dwarf again appeared and asked, for the third time, 'What will you give me to do this for you?'

'I have nothing left that I can give you,' replied the maiden.

'Then promise me your first-born child if you become Queen,' said he.

The Miller's daughter thought, 'Who can tell if that will ever happen?' and, ignorant how else to help herself out of her trouble, she promised the Dwarf what he desired; and he immediately set about and finished the spinning. When morning came, and the King found all he had wished for done, he celebrated his wedding, and the Miller's fair daughter became Queen.

The gay times she had at the King's Court caused her to forget that she had made a very foolish promise.

About a year after the marriage, when she had ceased to think about the little Dwarf, she brought a fine child into the world; and, suddenly, soon after its birth, the very man appeared and demanded what she had promised. The frightened Queen offered him all the riches of the kingdom if he would leave her her child; but the Dwarf answered, 'No; something human is dearer to me than all the wealth of the world.'

The Queen began to weep and groan so much that the Dwarf pitied her, and said, 'I will leave you three days to consider; if you in that time discover my name you shall keep your child.'

All night long the Queen racked her brains for all the names she could think of, and sent a messenger through the country to collect far and wide any new names. The following morning came the Dwarf, and she began with 'Caspar,'

'Melchior,' 'Balthassar,' and all the odd names she knew; but at each the little Man exclaimed, 'That is not my name.' The second day the Queen inquired of all her people for uncommon and curious names, and called the Dwarf 'Ribs-of-Beef,' 'Sheep- shank,' 'Whalebone,' but at each he said, 'This is not my name.'

The third day the messenger came back and said, 'I have not found a single name; but as I came to a high mountain near the edge of a forest, where foxes and hares say good night to each other, I saw there a little house, and before the door a fire was burning, and round this fire a very curious little Man was dancing on one leg, and shouting:

"To-day I stew, and then I'll bake,
Tomorrow I shall the Queen's child take;

Ah! how famous it is that nobody knows
That my name is Rumpelstiltskin."

When the Queen heard this she was very glad, for now she knew the name; and soon after came the Dwarf, and asked,

'Now, my lady Queen, what is my name?'

First she said, 'Are you called Conrade?'

'No.'

'Are you called Hal?'

'No.'

'Are you called Rumpelstiltskin?'

'A witch has told you! a witch has told you!' shrieked the little Man, and stamped his right foot so hard in the ground with rage that he could not draw it out again. Then he took hold of his left leg with both his hands, and pulled away so hard that his right came off in the struggle, and he hopped away howling terribly.

And from that day to this the Queen has heard no more of her troublesome visitor.

7

Eva's Visit to Fairyland

A little girl lay on the grass down by the brook wondering what the brown water said as it went babbling over the stones. As she listened she heard another kind of music that seemed to come nearer and nearer, till round the corner floated a beautiful boat filled with elves, who danced on the broad green leaves of the lily of the valley, while the white bells of the tall stem that was the mast rung loud and sweet.

A flat rock, covered with moss, stood in the middle of the brook, and here the boat was anchored for the elves to rest a little. Eva watched them at their pretty play, as they flew about or lay fanning themselves and drinking from the red-brimmed cups on the rocks. Wild strawberries grew in the grass close by, and Eva threw some of the ripest to the fairy folk; for honey and dew seemed a poor sort of lunch to the child. Then the elves saw her, and nodded and smiled and called, but their soft voices could not reach her. So, after whispering among themselves, two of them flew to the brookside, and perching on a buttercup said close to Eva's ear, 'We have come to thank you for your berries, and to ask if we can do anything for you, because this is our holiday and we can become visible to you.'

'Oh, let me go to Fairyland! I have longed so to see and know all about you dear little people and never would believe it is true that there are no fairies left,' cried Eva, so glad to find that she was right.

'We should not dare to take some children, they would do so much harm; but you believe in us, you love all the sweet things in the world, and never hurt innocent creatures, or tread on flowers, or let ugly passions come into your happy little heart. You shall go with us and see how we live.'

But as the elves spoke, Eva looked very sad and said, 'How can I go? I am so big I should sink that pretty ship with one finger, and I have no wings.'

The elves laughed and touched her with their soft hands, saying, 'You cannot hurt us now. Look in the water and see what we have done.'

Eva looked and saw a tiny child standing under a tall blue violet. It was herself, but so small she seemed an elf in a white pinafore and little pink sun-bonnet. She clapped her hands and skipped for joy, and laughed at the cunning picture; but suddenly she grew sober again, as she looked from the shore to the rock.

'But now I am so wee I cannot step over, and you cannot lift me, I am sure.'

'Give us each a hand and do not be afraid,' said the elves, and whisked her across like dandelion down.

The elves were very glad to see her, and touched and peeped and asked questions as if they had never had a mortal child to play with before. Eva was so small she could dance with them now, and eat what they ate, and sing their pretty songs. She found that flower-honey and dewdrops were very nice, and that it was fine fun to tilt on a blade of grass, to slide down a smooth bulrush-stem, or rock in the cup of a flower. She learned new and merry games, found out what the brook said, saw a cowslip blossom, and had a lovely time till the captain of the ship blew a long sweet blast on a honeysuckle horn, and all the elves went aboard and set sail for home.

'Now I shall find the way to Fairyland and can go again whenever I like,' thought Eva, as she floated away.

But the sly little people did not mean that she should know, for only now and then can a child go to that lovely place. So they set the bells to chiming softly, and all sung lullabies till Eva fell fast asleep, and knew nothing of the journey till she woke in Fairyland.

It seemed to be sunset; for the sky was red, the flowers all dreaming behind their green curtains, the birds tucked up in their nests, and there was no sound but the whisper of the wind that softly sang, 'Good-night, good-night.'

'We all go early to bed unless the moon shines. We are

tired, so come and let us make you cosey till to-morrow,' said the elves, showing her a dainty bed with white rose-leaves for sheets, a red rose-leaf for coverlet, and two plump little mushrooms for pillows. Cobweb curtains hung over it, a glow-worm was the candle, and a lily-of-the-valley cup made a nice night-cap, while a tiny gown of woven thistle-down lay ready to be put on.

Eva quickly undressed and slipped into the pretty bed, where she lay looking at the red light till sleep kissed her eyelids, and a lovely dream floated through her mind till morning came.

As soon as the sun peeped over the hills the elves were up and away to the lake, where they all dipped and splashed and floated and frolicked till the air was full of sparkling drops and the water white with foam. Then they wiped on soft cobweb towels, which they spread on the grass to dry, while they combed their pretty hair and put on fresh gowns of flower-leaves. After that came breakfast, all sitting about in parties to eat fruit and cakes of pollen, while their drink was fresh dew.

'Now, Eva, you see that we are not idle, foolish creatures, but have many things to do, many lessons to learn, and a heaven of our own to hope for,' said the elves when they had all sung together; while the wind, who was the house-maid there, cleared the tables by blowing everything away at one breath. 'First of all come to our hospital,—for here we bring all the sick and hurt things cruel or careless people have harmed. In your world children often torment and kill poor birds and worms and flies, and pick flowers to throw away, and chase butterflies till their poor wings are broken. All these we care for, and our magic makes them live again. Come and see.'

Eva followed to a cool, quiet place, where on soft beds lay many wounded things. Rose, the fairy nurse, was binding up the leg of a fly as he lay in a cobweb hammock and feebly buzzed his thanks. In another place an ugly worm was being put together after a cruel boy had cut him in two. Eva thought the elves were good to do such work, and went on to a humming- bird which lay in a bed of honeysuckles, with the quick colours very dim on its little breast and bright wings very still.

'I was shot with an air-gun, and my poor head still aches with the dreadful blow,' sighed the poor bird, trying to sip a little honey with his long beak.

'I'm nearly well,' chirped a cricket, whose stiff tail had been pulled off by a naughty child and nicely put on again by a very skilful elf.

He looked so cheerful and lively as he hopped about on his bed of dried grass, with his black eyes twinkling, and a bandage of bindweed holding his tail firmly in place till it was well, that Eva laughed aloud, and at the pleasant sound all the sick things smiled and seemed better.

Rows of pale flowers stood in one place, and elves watered them, or tied up broken leaves, or let in the sunshine to cure their pains,—for these delicate invalids needed much care; and

Mignonette was the name of the nurse who watched

over them, like a little Sister of Charity, with her grey gown and sweet face.

'You have seen enough. Come to school now, and see where we are taught all that fairies must know,' said Trip, the elf who was guiding her about.

In a pleasant place they found the child elves sitting on pink daisies with their books of leaves in their hands, while the teacher was a Jack-in-the-pulpit, who asked questions, and was very wise. Eva nodded to the little ones, and they smiled at the stranger as they rustled their books and pretended to study busily.

A class in arithmetic was going on, and Eva listened to questions that none but elves would care to know.

'Twinkle, if there were fifteen seeds on a dandelion, and the wind blew ten away, how many would be left?'

'Five.'

'Bud, if a rose opens three leaves one day, two the next, and seven the next, how many in all?'

'Eleven.'

'Daisy, if a silk-worm spins one yard of fairy cloth in an hour, how many can he spin in a day?'

'Twelve, if he isn't lazy,' answered the little elf, fluttering her wings, as if anxious to be done.

'Now we will read,' said Jack, and a new class flew to the long leaf, where they stood in a row, with open books, ready to begin.

'You may read The Flower's Lesson to-day, and be careful not to sing-song, Poppy,' said the teacher, passing a dainty book to Eva that she might follow the story.

'Once there was a rose who had two little buds. One was happy and contented, but the other always wanted something.

"I wish the elves would bring me a star instead of dew every night. The drop is soon gone, but a star would shine splendidly, and I should be finer than all the other flowers, said the naughty bud one night.

"But you need the dew to live, and the moon needs the stars up there to light the world. Don't fret, sister, but be sure it is best to take what is sent, and be glad, answered the good bud.

"I won't have the dew, and if I cannot get a star I will take a firefly to shine on my breast, said the other, shaking off a fresh drop that had just fallen on her, and folding her leaves round the bright fly.

'Foolish child! cried the rose-mother; let the fly go, before he harms you. It is better to be sweet and fair than to shine with a beauty not your own. Be wise, dear, before it is too late.

'But the silly bud only held the firefly closer, till in its struggles it tore her leaves and flew away. When the hot sun came up the poor bud hung all faded on her stem, longing for a cool drop to drink. Her sister was strong and fresh, and danced gayly in the wind, opening her red petals to the sun.

"Now I must die. Oh, why was I vain and silly? sobbed the poor bud, fainting in the heat.

'Then the mother leaned over her, and from her bosom, where she had hidden it, the dew-drop fell on the thirsty bud, and while she drank it eagerly the rose drew her closer, whispering, Little darling, learn to be contented with what heaven sends, and make yourself lovely by being good."'

'I shall remember that story,' said Eva when the elves shut their books and flew back to the daisy seats.

'Would you like to hear them sing?' asked Trip.

'Very much,' said Eva, and in the little song they gave her she got another lesson to carry home.

'I shine,' says the sun,
'To give the world light,'
'I glimmer,' adds the moon,
'To beautify the night.'
'I ripple,' says the brook,
'I whisper,' sighs the breeze,
'I patter,' laughs the rain,
'We rustle,' call the trees
'We dance,' nod the daisies,
'I twinkle,' shines the star,
'We sing,' chant the birds,
'How happy we all are!'
'I smile,' cries the child,
Gentle, good, and gay;
The sweetest thing of all,
The sunshine of each day.

'I shall sing that to myself and try to do my part,' said Eva, as the elves got out their paints and brushes of butterfly-down, and using large white leaves for paper, learned to imitate the colours of every flower.

'Why do they do this?' asked Eva, for she saw no pictures anywhere.

'We keep the flowers fresh, for in the world below they have trials with the hot sun that fades, the mould that spots, grubs that gnaw, and frost that kills. We melt bits of rainbow in our paint-pots, and when it is needed we brighten the soft colour on Anemone's cheeks, deepen the blue of Violet's eyes, or polish up the cowslips till they shine like cups of gold. We redden the autumn leaves, and put the purple bloom on the grapes. We made the budding birches a soft green, colour maple keys, and hang brown tassels on the alder twigs. We repair the dim spots on butterflies' wings, paint the blue-bird like the sky, give Robin his red vest, and turn the yellow bird to a flash of sunshine. Oh, we are artists, and hereafter you will see our pictures everywhere.'

'How lovely!' said Eva. 'I often wondered who kept all these delicate things so beautiful and gay. But where are we going now?' she added, as the elves led her away from the school.

'Come and see where we learn to ride,' they answered, smiling as if they enjoyed this part of their education.

In a little dell where the ground was covered with the softest moss Eva found the fairy riding-school and gymnasium. The horses were all kinds of winged and swift-footed things, and the race-ground was a smooth path round the highest moss mound. Groups of elves lay on the ground, swung on the grass-blades, or sat in the wood flowers, that stood all about.

In one place the mothers and fathers were teaching their little ones to fly. The baby elves sat in a row on the branch of a birch-tree, fluttering their small wings and nestling close together, timid yet longing to launch boldly out into the air and float as the others did. The parents were very patient, and one by one the babies took little flights, getting braver and braver each time.

One very timid elf would not stir, so the sly papa and mamma put it on a leaf, and each taking a side, they rode the dear about for a few minutes, till she was used to the motion; then they dropped the leaf, and the little elf finding herself falling spread her wings and flew away to a tall bush, to the great delight of all who saw it.

But the riding was very funny, and Eva soon forgot everything else in watching the gay creatures mount their various horses and fly or gallop round the ring while the teacher—a small fellow in a gay cap and green suit—stood on the moss- mound, cracking a long whip and telling them how to ride in the best fairy fashion.

Several lady elves learned to mount butterflies gracefully and float where they liked, sitting firmly when the winged horses alighted on the flowers. The boy elves preferred field-mice, who went very swiftly round and round, with saddles of woven grass and reins of yellow bindweed, which looked well on the little grey creatures, who twinkled their bright eyes and whisked their long tails as if they liked it.

But the best fun of all was when the leaping began; and Eva quite trembled lest some sad accident should happen;

for grasshoppers were led out, and the gallant elves leaped over the highest flower-tops without falling off.

It was very funny to see the queer hoppers skip with their long legs, and when Puck, the riding-master, mounted, and led a dozen of his pupils a race round the track, all the rest of the elves laughed aloud and clapped their hands in great glee; for Puck was a famous fairy, and his pranks were endless.

Eva was shouting with the rest as the green horses came hopping by, when Puck caught her up before him, and away they raced so swiftly that her hair whistled in the wind and her breath was nearly gone. A tremendous leap took them high over the little hill and landed Eva in a tall dandelion, where she lay laughing and panting as if on a little yellow sofa, while Trip and her mates fanned her and smoothed her pretty hair.

'That was splendid!' she cried. 'I wish I was a real fairy, and always lived in this lovely place. Everything will seem so ugly and big and coarse when I go home I shall never be happy again.'

'Oh, yes, you will,' answered Trip, 'for after this visit you will be able to hear and see and know what others never do, and that will make you happy and good. You believed in us, and we reward all who love what we love, and enjoy the beautiful world they live in as we do.'

'Thank you,' said Eva. 'If I can know what the birds sing and the brook, and talk with the flowers, and see faces in the sky, and hear music in the wind, I won't mind being a child, even if people call me queer.'

'You shall understand many lovely things and be able to put them into tales and songs that all will read and sing and thank you for,' said Moonbeam, a sweet, thoughtful elf, who stole quietly about, and was always singing like a soft wind.

'Oh, that is what I always wanted to do,' cried Eva, 'for I love my song-books best, and never find new ones enough. Show me more, dear elves, so that I can have many fine tales to tell when I am old enough to write.'

'Come, then, and see our sweetest sight. We cannot show it to every one, but your eyes will be able to see through the veil, and you will understand the meaning of our flower-heaven.'

So Moonlight led her away from all the rest, along a little winding path that went higher and higher till they stood on a hilltop.

'Look up and follow me,' said the elf, and touching Eva's shoulders with her wand, a pair of wings shot out, and away she floated after her guide toward what looked like a white cloud sailing in the blue sky.

When they alighted a soft mist was round them, and through it Eva saw a golden glimmer like sunshine.

'Look, but do not speak,' said Moonlight, beckoning her along.

Soon the mist passed away and nothing but a thin veil of gossamer like a silken cobweb hung between them and the world beyond. 'Can you see through it?' whispered the elf anxiously.

Eva nodded, and then forgot everything to look with all her eyes into a lovely land of flowers; for the walls were of white lilies, the trees were rose-trees, the ground blue violets, and the birds the little yellow canary-plant, whose blossoms are like birds on the wing. Columbines sounded their red horns, and the air was filled with delicate voices, unlike any ever heard before, because it was the sweet breath of flowers set to music.

But what surprised Eva most was the sight of a common dandelion, a tuft of clover, a faded mignonette-plant, with several other humble flowers, set in a little plot by themselves as if newly come, and about them gathered a crowd of beautiful spirits, so bright, so small, so perfect that Eva could hardly see them, and winked as if dazzled by the sunshine of this garden among the clouds.

'Who are they? and why do they care for those poor flowers?' whispered Eva, forgetting that she must not speak.

Before Moonlight could answer, all grew dim for a moment, as if a cold breath had passed beyond the curtain and chilled the delicate world within.

'Hush! mortal voices must not be heard here,' answered the elf with a warning look.

'These lovely creatures are the spirits of flowers who did some good deed when they bloomed on earth, and their reward is to live here forever where there is no frost, no rain, no stormy wind to hurt them. Those poor plants have just come, for their work is done, and their souls will soon be set free from the shapes that hold them. You will see how beautiful they have made themselves when out of the common flowers come souls like the perfect ones who are welcoming them.

'That dandelion lived in the room of a poor little sick girl who had no other toy, no other playmate. She watched and loved it as she lay on her bed, for she was never well, and the good flower, instead of fading without sunshine in that dreary room, bloomed its best, till it shone like a little sun. The child died with it in her hand, and when she no longer needed it, we saved it from being thrown away and brought it here to live forever.

'The clover grew in a prison-yard, and a bad boy shut up there watched it as the only green thing that made him think of the fields at home where his mother was waiting and hoping he would come back to her. Clover did her best to keep good thoughts in his mind and he loved her, and tried to repent, and when he was told he might go, he meant to take his flower with him but forgot it in his hurry to get home. We did not forget, for the wind that goes everywhere had told us the little story, and we brought brave Clover out of prison to this flower-heaven.

'Mignonette lived in a splendid garden, but no one minded her, for she is only a little brown thing and hid in a corner, happy with her share of sunshine and rain, and her daily task of blossoming green and strong. People admired the other fine flowers and praised their perfume, never knowing that the sweetest breath of all came from the nook where Mignonette modestly hid behind the roses. No one ever praised her, or came to watch her, and the gardener took no care of her. But the bees found her out and came every day to sip her sweet honey, the butterflies loved her better than the proud roses, and the wind always stopped for a kiss as it flew by. When autumn came and all the other plants were done blossoming, and stood bare and faded, there was modest Mignonette still green and fresh, still with a blossom or two, and still smiling contentedly with a bosom full of ripened seeds,—her summer work well done, her happy heart ready for the winter sleep.

'But we said, "No frost shall touch our brave flower; she shall not be neglected another year, but come to live loved and honoured in the eternal summer that shines here." Now look.'

Eva brushed away the tears that had filled her eyes as she listened to these little histories, and looking eagerly, saw how from the dandelion, set free by the spells the spirits sang, there rose, light as down, a little golden soul, in the delicate shape the others wore. One in pale rose came from the clover, and a third in soft green with dusky wings; but a bright face flew out of the mignonette. Then the others took hands and floated round the new-comers in an airy dance, singing so joyfully that Eva clapped her hands crying, 'Happy souls! I will go home and try to be as good as they were; then I may be as happy when I go away to my heaven.'

The sound of her voice made all dark, and she would have been frightened if the elf had not taken her hand and led her back to the edge of the cloud, saying as they flew down to Fairyland—'See, the sun is setting; we must take you home before this midsummer day ends, and with it our power to make ourselves known.'

Eva had so much to tell that she was ready to go; but a new surprise waited for her, and she saw a fairy spectacle as she came again before the palace.

Banners of gay tulip-leaves were blowing in the wind from the lances of reeds held by a troop of elves mounted on mice; a car made of a curled green leaf with checkerberry wheels and cushions of pink mushrooms stood ready for her, and Trip as maid of honour helped her in. Lady elves on butterflies flew behind, and the Queen's trumpeters marched before making music on their horns. All the people of Elfland lined the way, throwing flowers, waving their hands, and calling, 'Farewell, little Eva! Come again! Do not forget us!' till she was out of sight.

'How sweet and kind you are to me. What can I do to thank you?' said Eva to Trip, who sat beside her as they rolled along,—a gay and lovely sight, if any but fairy eyes could have seen it.

'Remember all you have seen and heard. Love the good and beautiful things you will find everywhere, and be always a happy child at heart,' answered Trip with a kiss.

Before Eva could speak the sun set and in a moment every elf was invisible, all the pretty show was gone, and the child stood alone by the brook. But she never forgot her visit to Fairyland, and as she grew up she seemed to be a sort of elf herself, happy, gay, and good, with the power of making every one love her as she went singing and smiling through the world. She wrote songs that people loved to sing, told tales children delighted to read, and found so much wisdom, beauty and music everywhere, that it was very plain she understood the sweet language of bird and flower, wind and water, and remembered all the lessons the elves taught her.

8

The Sleeping Beauty in the Wood

Once there was a royal couple who grieved excessively because they had no children. When at last, after long waiting, the queen presented her husband with a little daughter, his majesty showed his joy by giving a christening feast so grand that the like of it was never known. He invited all the fairies in the land—there were seven altogether—to stand godmothers to the little princess, hoping that each might bestow on her some good gift, as was the custom of good fairies in those days.

After the ceremony all the guests returned to the palace, where there was set before each fairy-godmother a magnificent covered dish, with an embroidered table-napkin and a knife and fork of pure gold studded with diamonds and rubies. But alas! as they placed themselves at table there entered an old fairy who had never been invited, because more than fifty years since she had left the king's dominion on a tour of pleasure and had not been heard of until this day. His majesty, much troubled, desired a cover to be placed for her, but it was of common delf, for he had ordered from his jeweller only seven gold dishes for the seven fairies aforesaid. The elderly fairy thought herself neglected, and muttered angry menaces, which were overheard by one of the younger fairies, who chanced to sit beside her. This good godmother, afraid of harm to the pretty baby, hastened to hide herself behind the tapestry in the hall. She did this because she wished all the others to speak first—so that if any ill gift were bestowed on the child she might be able to counteract it.

The six now offered their good wishes—which, unlike most wishes, were sure to come true. The fortunate little princess was to grow up the fairest woman in the world; to have a temper sweet as an angel; to be perfectly graceful and gracious; to sing like a nightingale; to dance like a leaf on a tree; and to possess every accomplishment under the sun. Then the old fairy's turn came. Shaking her head spitefully, she uttered the wish that when the baby grew up into a young lady, and learned to spin, she might prick her finger with the spindle and die of the wound.

At this terrible prophecy all the guests shuddered, and some of the more tender-hearted began to weep. The lately happy parents were almost out of their wits with grief. Upon which the wise young fairy appeared from behind the tapestry, saying cheerfully; 'Your majesties may comfort yourselves;

the princess shall not die. I have no power to alter the ill-fortune just wished her by my ancient sister—her finger must be pierced, and she shall then sink, not into the sleep of death, but into a sleep that will last a hundred years. After that time is ended the son of a king will find her, awaken her, and marry her.'

Immediately all the fairies vanished.

The king, in the hope of avoiding his daughter's doom, issued an edict forbidding all persons to spin, and even to have spinning-wheels in their houses, on pain of instant death. But it was in vain. One day, when she was just fifteen years of age, the king and queen left their daughter alone in one of their castles, when, wandering about at her will, she came to an ancient dungeon tower, climbed to the top of it, and there found a very old woman—so old and deaf that she had never heard of the king's edict—busy with her wheel.

'What are you doing, good old woman?' said the princess.

'I'm spinning, my pretty child.'

'Ah, how charming! Let me try if I can spin also.'

She had no sooner taken up the spindle than, being lively and obstinate, she handled it so awkwardly and carelessly that the point pierced her finger. Though it was so small a wound, she fainted away at once, and dropped silently down on the floor. The poor, frightened old woman called for help; shortly came the ladies in waiting, who tried every means to restore their young mistress, but all their care was useless. She lay, beautiful as an angel, the colour still lingering in her lips and cheeks; her fair bosom softly stirred with her breath;

only her eyes were fast closed. When the king, her father, and the queen, her mother, beheld her thus, they knew regret was idle—all had happened as the cruel fairy meant. But they also knew that their daughter would not sleep forever, though after one hundred years it was not likely they would either of them behold her awakening. Until that happy hour should arrive, they determined to leave her in repose. They sent away all the physicians and attendants, and themselves sorrowfully laid her upon a bed of embroidery, in the most elegant apartment of the palace. There she slept and looked like a sleeping angel still.

When this misfortune happened, the kindly young fairy who had saved the princess by changing her sleep of death into this sleep of a hundred years was twelve thousand leagues away in the kingdom of Mataquin. But being informed of everything, she arrived speedily in a chariot of fire drawn by dragons. The king was somewhat startled by the sight, but nevertheless went to the door of his palace, and, with a mournful countenance, presented her his hand to descend.

The fairy condoled with his majesty, and approved of all he had done. Then, being a fairy of great common-sense and foresight, she suggested that the princess, awakening after a hundred years in this ancient castle, might be a good deal embarrassed, especially with a young prince by her side, to find herself alone. Accordingly, without asking any one's leave, she touched with her magic wand the entire population of the palace, except the king and queen—governesses, ladies of honour, waiting-maids, gentlemen ushers, cooks, kitchen-girls, pages, footmen, down to the horses that were in the stables and the grooms that attended them—she touched each and all. Nay, with kind consideration for the feelings of the princess, she even touched the little fat lapdog Puffy, who had laid himself down beside his mistress on her splendid bed. He, like all the rest, fell fast asleep in a moment. The very spits that were before the kitchen fire ceased turning, and the fire itself went out, and everything became as silent as if it were the middle of the night, or as if the palace were a palace of the dead.

The king and queen—having kissed their daughter and wept over her a little, but not much, she looked so sweet and content—departed from the castle, giving orders that it was to be approached no more. The command was unnecessary; for in one quarter of an hour there sprung up around it a wood so thick and thorny that neither beasts nor men could attempt to penetrate there. Above this dense mass of forest could only be perceived the top of the high tower where the lovely princess slept.

A great many changes happen in a hundred years. The king, who never had a second child, died, and his throne passed into another royal family. So entirely was the story of the poor princess forgotten, that when the reigning king's son, being one day out hunting and stopped in the chase by this formidable wood, inquired what wood it was, and what were those towers which he saw appearing out of the midst of it, no one could answer him. At length an old peasant was found who remembered having heard his grandfather say to his father, that in this tower was a princess, beautiful as the day, who was doomed to sleep there for one hundred years, until awakened by a king's son, her destined bridegroom.

At this the young prince, who had the spirit of a hero, determined to find out the truth for himself. Spurred on by both generosity and curiosity, he leaped from his horse and began to force his way through the thick wood. To his amazement the stiff branches all gave way, and the ugly thorns sheathed themselves of their own accord, and the brambles buried themselves in the earth to let him pass. This done, they closed behind him, allowing none of his suite to follow: but, ardent and young, he went boldly on alone. The first thing he saw was enough to smite him with fear. Bodies of men and horses lay extended on the ground; but the men had faces, not death-white, but red as peonies, and beside them were glasses half filled with wine, showing that they had gone to sleep drinking. Next he entered a large court paved with marble, where stood rows of guards presenting arms, but motionless as if cut out of stone; then he passed through many chambers where gentlemen and ladies, all in the costume of the past century, slept at their ease, some standing, some sitting. The pages were lurking in corners, the ladies of honour were stooping over their embroidery frames, or listening apparently with polite attention to the gentlemen of the court, but all were as silent as statues and as immovable. Their clothes, strange to say, were fresh and new as ever; and not a particle of dust or spider-web had gathered over the furniture, though it had not known a broom for a hundred years. Finally the astonished prince came to an inner chamber, where was the fairest sight his eyes had ever beheld.

A young girl of wonderful beauty lay asleep on an embroidered bed, and she looked as if she had only just closed her eyes. Trembling, the prince approached and knelt beside her. Some say he kissed her, but as nobody saw it, and she never told, we cannot be quite sure of the fact. However, as the end of the enchantment had come, the princess awakened at once, and, looking at him with eyes of the tenderest regard, said, drowsily: 'Is it you, my prince? I have waited for you very long.'

Charmed with these words, and still more with the tone in which they were uttered, the prince assured her that he loved her more than his life. Nevertheless, he was the most embarrassed of the two; for, thanks to the kind fairy, the princess had plenty of time to dream of him during her century of slumber, while he had never even heard of her till an hour before. For a long time did they sit conversing, and yet had not said half enough. Their only interruption was the little dog Puffy, who had awakened with his mistress, and now began to be exceedingly jealous that the princess did not notice him as much as she was wont to do.

Meantime all the attendants, whose enchantment was also broken, not being in love, were ready to die of hunger after their fast of a hundred years. A lady of honour ventured to intimate that dinner was served; whereupon the prince handed his beloved princess at once to the great hall. She did not wait to dress for dinner, being already perfectly and magnificently attired, though in a fashion somewhat out of date. However, her lover had the politeness not to notice this, nor to remind her that she was dressed exactly like her royal grandmother, whose portrait still hung on the palace walls.

During the banquet a concert took place by the attendant musicians, and considering they had not touched their instruments for a century, they played extremely well. They ended with a wedding march; for that very evening the marriage of the prince and princess was celebrated, and though the bride was nearly one hundred years older than the bridegroom, it is remarkable that the fact would never had been discovered by any one unacquainted therewith.

After a few days they went together out of the castle and enchanted wood, both of which immediately vanished, and were never more beheld by mortal eyes. The princess was restored to her ancestral kingdom, but it was not generally declared who she was, as during a hundred years people had grown so very much cleverer that nobody then living would ever have believed the story. So nothing was explained, and nobody presumed to ask any questions about her, for ought not a prince be able to marry whomsoever he pleases?

Nor—whether or not the day of fairies was over—did the princess ever see anything further of her seven godmothers. She lived a long and happy life, like any other ordinary woman, and died at length, beloved, regretted, but, the prince being already no more, perfectly contented.

9

Jack and the Bean-Stalk

In the days of King Alfred there lived a poor woman whose cottage was in a remote country village many miles from London. She had been a widow some years, and had an only child named Jack, whom she indulged so much that he never paid the least attention to anything she said, but was indolent, careless and extravagant. His follies were not owing to a bad disposition, but to his mother's foolish partiality. By degrees he spent all that she had—scarcely anything remained but a cow.

One day, for the first time in her life, she reproached him: 'Cruel, cruel boy! you have at last brought me to beggary. I have not money enough to purchase even a bit of bread; nothing now remains to sell but my poor cow! I am sorry to part with her; it grieves me sadly, but we cannot starve.' For a few minutes Jack felt remorse, but it was soon over; and he began asking his mother to let him sell the cow at the next village, teasing her so much that she at last consented.

As he was going along he met a butcher, who inquired why he was driving the cow from home? Jack replied he was going to sell it. The butcher held some curious beans in his hat; they were of various colours and attracted Jack's attention. This did not pass unnoticed by the man, who, knowing Jack's easy temper, thought now was the time to take an advantage of it, and, determined not to let slip so good an opportunity, asked what was the price of the cow, offering at the same time all the beans in his hat for her. The silly boy could not conceal the pleasure he felt at what he supposed so great an offer; the bargain was struck instantly, and the cow exchanged for a few paltry beans. Jack made the best of his way home, calling aloud to his mother before he reached the door, thinking to surprise her.

When she saw the beans and heard Jack's account, her patience quite forsook her; she tossed the beans out of the window, where they fell on the garden-bed below. Then she threw her apron over her head and cried bitterly. Jack attempted to console her, but in vain, and, not having anything to eat, they both went supperless to bed. Jack awoke early in the morning, and, seeing something uncommon darkening the window of his bedchamber, ran down-stairs into the garden, where he found some of the beans had taken root and sprung up surprisingly; the stalks were of an immense thickness, and had twined together until they formed a ladder like a chain, and so high that the top appeared to be lost in the clouds. Jack was an adventurous lad; he determined to climb up to the top, and ran to tell his mother, not doubting but that she would be as much pleased as he was. She declared he should not go, said it would break her heart if he did—entreated and threatened, but all in vain. Jack set out, and after climbing for some hours reached the top of the bean-stalk quite exhausted. Looking around, he found himself in a strange country; it appeared to be a barren desert— not a tree, shrub, house or living creature was to be seen; here and there were scattered fragments of stone; and at unequal distances small heaps of earth were loosely thrown together.

Jack seated himself pensively upon a block of stone and thought of his mother; he reflected with sorrow upon his disobedience in climbing the bean-stalk against her will, and concluded that he must die of hunger. However, he walked on, hoping to see a house where he might beg something to eat and drink. He did not find it; but he saw at a distance a beautiful lady, walking all alone. She was elegantly clad and carried a white wand, at the top of which sat a peacock of pure gold.

Jack, who was a gallant fellow, went straight up to her, when, with a bewitching smile, she asked him how he came there. He told her all about the bean-stalk. The lady answered him by a question, 'Do you remember your father, young man?'

'No, madam; but I am sure there is some mystery about him, for when I name him to my mother she always begins to weep, and will tell me nothing.'

'She dare not,' replied the lady, 'but I can and will. For know, young man, that I am a fairy and was your father's guardian. But fairies are bound by laws as well as mortals, and by an error of mine I lost my power for a term of years, so that I was unable to succour your father when he most needed it, and he died.' Here the fairy looked so sorrowful that Jack's heart warmed to her, and he begged her earnestly to tell him more.

'I will; only you must promise to obey me in everything, or you will perish yourself.'

Jack was brave, and, besides, his fortunes were so bad they could not well be worse, so he promised.

The fairy continued: 'Your father, Jack, was a most excellent, amiable, generous man. He had a good wife, faithful servants, plenty of money; but he had one misfortune—a false friend. This was a giant, whom he had succoured in misfortune, and who returned his kindness by murdering him, and seizing on all his property; also making your mother take a solemn oath that she would never tell you anything about your father, or he would murder both her and you. Then he turned her off with you in her arms, to wander about the wide world as she might. I could not help her, as my power only returned on the day you went to sell your cow.

'It was I,' added the fairy, 'who impelled you to take the beans, who made the bean-stalk grow, and inspired you with the desire to climb up it to this strange country; for it is here the wicked giant lives who was your father's destroyer. It is you who must avenge him, and rid the world of a monster who never will do anything but evil. I will assist you. You may lawfully take possession of his house and all his riches, for everything he has belonged to your father, and is therefore yours. Now farewell! Do not let your mother know you are acquainted with your father's history. This is my command, and if you disobey me you will suffer for it. Now go.'

Jack asked where he was to go.

'Along the direct road till you see the house where the giant lives. You must then act according to your own just judgement, and I will guide you if any difficulty arises. Farewell!'

She bestowed on the youth a benignant smile, and vanished. Jack pursued his journey. He walked on till after sunset, when to his great joy, he espied a large mansion. A plain-looking woman was at the door; he accosted her, begging she would give him a morsel of bread and a night's lodging. She expressed the greatest surprise, and said it was quite uncommon to see a human being near their house; for it was well known that her husband was a powerful giant, who would never eat anything but human flesh, if he could possibly get it; that he would walk fifty miles to procure it, usually being out the whole day for that purpose.

This account greatly terrified Jack, but still he hoped to elude the giant, and therefore he again entreated the woman to take him in for one night only, and hide him where she thought proper. She at last suffered herself to be persuaded, for she was of a compassionate and generous disposition, and took him into the house. First they entered a fine large hall magnificently furnished; they then passed through several spacious rooms in the same style of grandeur; but all appeared forsaken and desolate. A long gallery came next; it was very dark—just light enough to show that, instead of a wall on one side, there was a grating of iron which parted off a dismal dungeon, from whence issued the groans of those victims whom the cruel giant reserved in confinement for his own voracious appetite.

Poor Jack was half dead with fear, and would have given the world to have been with his mother again, for he now began to doubt if he should ever see her more; he even mistrusted the good woman, and thought she had let him into the house for no other purpose than to lock him up among the unfortunate people in the dungeon. However, she bade Jack sit down, and gave him plenty to eat and drink; and he, not seeing anything to make him uncomfortable, soon forgot his fear and was just beginning to enjoy himself, when he was startled by a loud knocking at the outer door, which made the whole house shake.

'Ah! that's the giant; and if he sees you he will kill you and me, too,' cried the poor woman, trembling all over. 'What shall I do?'

'Hide me in the oven,' cried Jack, now as bold as a lion at the thought of being face to face with his father's cruel murderer. So he crept into the oven—for there was no fire near it—and listened to the giant's loud voice and heavy step as he went up and down the kitchen scolding his wife. At last he seated himself at table, and Jack, peeping through a crevice in the oven, was amazed to see what a quantity of food he devoured. It seemed as if he never would have done eating and drinking; but he did at last, and, leaning back, called to his wife in a voice like thunder:

'Bring me my hen!'

She obeyed, and placed upon the table a very beautiful live hen.

'Lay!' roared the giant, and the hen laid immediately an egg of solid gold.

'Lay another!' and every time the giant said this the hen laid a larger egg than before.

He amused himself a long time with his hen, and then sent his wife to bed, while he fell asleep by the fireside and snored like the roaring of cannon.

As soon as he was asleep Jack crept out of the oven, seized the hen, and ran off with her. He got safely out of the house, and, finding his way along the road he came, reached the top of the bean-stalk, which he descended in safety.

His mother was overjoyed to see him. She thought he had come to some ill end.

'Not a bit of it, mother. Look here!' and he showed her the hen. 'Now lay,' and the hen obeyed him as readily as the giant, and laid as many golden eggs as he desired.

These eggs being sold, Jack and his mother got plenty of money, and for some months lived very happily together, till Jack got another great longing to climb the bean-stalk and carry away some more of the giant's riches. He had told his mother of his adventure, but had been very careful not to say a word about his father. He thought of his journey again and again, but still he could not summon resolution enough to break it to his mother, being well assured that she would endeavour to prevent his going. However, one day he told her boldly that he must take another journey up the bean-stalk. She begged and prayed him not to think of it, and tried all in her power to dissuade him; she told him that the giant's wife would certainly know him again, and that the giant would desire nothing better than to get him into his power, that he might put him to a cruel death, in order to be revenged for the loss of his hen. Jack, finding that all his arguments were useless, ceased speaking, though resolved to go at all events. He had a dress prepared which would disguise him, and something to colour his skin; he thought it impossible for any one to recollect him in this dress.

A few mornings after he rose very early, and, unperceived by any one, climbed the bean-stalk a second time. He was greatly fatigued when he reached the top, and very hungry. Having rested some time on one of the stones, he pursued his journey to the giant's mansion, which he reached late in the evening. The woman was at the door as before. Jack addressed her, at the same time telling her a pitiful tale, and requesting that she would give him some victuals and drink, and also a night's lodging.

She told him (what he knew before very well) about her husband's being a powerful and cruel giant, and also that she had one night admitted a poor, hungry, friendless boy; that the little ungrateful fellow had stolen one of the giant's treasures, and ever since that her husband had been worse than before, using her very cruelly, and continually upbraiding her with being the cause of his misfortune. Jack felt sorry for her, but confessed nothing, and did his best to persuade her to admit him, but found it a very hard task. At last she consented, and as she led the way, Jack observed that everything was just as he had found it before. She took him into the kitchen, and after he had done eating and drinking, she hid him in an old lumber-closet. The giant returned at the usual time, and walked in so heavily that the house was shaken to its foundation. He seated himself by the fire, and soon after exclaimed, 'Wife, I smell fresh meat!'

The wife replied it was the crows which had brought a piece of raw meat and left it at the top of the house. While supper was preparing, the giant was very ill-tempered and impatient, frequently lifting up his hand to strike his wife for not being quick enough. He was also continually upbraiding her with the loss of his wonderful hen.

At last, having ended his supper, he cried, 'Give me something to amuse me—my harp or my money-bags.'

'Which will you have, my dear?' said the wife, humbly.

'My money-bags, because they are the heaviest to carry,' thundered he.

She brought them, staggering under the weight—two bags, one filled with new guineas and the other with new shillings. She emptied them out on the table, and the giant began counting them in great glee. 'Now you may go to bed, you old fool.' So the wife crept away.

Jack from his hiding-place watched the counting of the money, which he knew was his poor father's, and wished it was his own; it would give him much less trouble than going about selling the golden eggs. The giant, little thinking he was so narrowly observed, reckoned it all up, and then replaced it in the two bags, which he tied up very carefully and put beside his chair, with his little dog to guard them.

At last he fell asleep as before, and snored so loud that Jack compared his noise to the roaring of the sea in a high wind, when the tide is coming in. At last Jack, concluding all secure, stole out, in order to carry off the two bags of money; but just as he laid his hand upon one of them, the little dog, which he had not perceived before, started from under the giant's chair and barked most furiously. Instead of endeavouring to escape, Jack stood still, though expecting his enemy to awake every instant.

Contrary, however, to his expectation, the giant continued in a sound sleep, and Jack, seeing a piece of meat, threw it to the dog, who at once ceased barking and began to devour it. So Jack carried off the bags, one on each shoulder, but they were so heavy that it took him two whole days to descend the bean-stalk and get back to his mother's door.

When he came he found the cottage deserted. He ran from one room to another without being able to find any one; he then hastened into the village, hoping to see some of the neighbours, who could inform him where he could find his mother. An old woman at last directed him to a neighbouring house, where she was ill of a fever. He was greatly shocked at finding her apparently dying, and blamed himself bitterly as the cause of it all. However, at sight of her dear son, the poor woman revived and slowly recovered her health. Jack gave her his two money-bags. They had the cottage rebuilt and well furnished, and lived happier than they had ever done before.

For three years Jack heard no more of the bean-stalk, but he could not forget it, though he feared making his mother unhappy. It was in vain endeavouring to amuse himself; he became thoughtful, and would arise at the first dawn of day, and sit looking at the bean-stalk for hours together. His mother saw that something preyed upon his mind, and endeavoured to discover the cause; but Jack knew too well what the consequence would be should she succeed. He did his utmost, therefore, to conquer the great desire he had for another journey up the bean-stalk. Finding, however, that his inclination grew too powerful for him, he began to make secret preparations for his journey. He prepared a new disguise, better and more complete than the former, and when summer came, on the longest day he awoke as soon as it was light, and, without telling his mother, ascended the bean-stalk. He found the road, journey, etc., much as it was on the two former times. He arrived at the giant's mansion in the evening, and found the wife standing, as usual, at the door. Jack had disguised himself so completely that she did not appear to have the least recollection of him; however, when he pleaded hunger and poverty, in order to gain admittance, he found it very difficult indeed to persuade her. At last he prevailed, and was concealed in the copper. When the giant returned he said, furiously, 'I smell fresh meat!' But Jack felt quite composed, since the giant had said this before and had been soon satisfied. However, the giant started up suddenly, and, notwithstanding all his wife could say, he searched all round the room. While this was going forward Jack was exceedingly terrified, wishing himself at home a thousand times; but when the giant approached the copper and put his hand upon the lid, Jack thought his death was certain.

But nothing happened; for the giant did not take the trouble to lift up the lid, but sat down shortly by the fireside and began to eat his enormous supper. When he had finished he commanded his wife to fetch down his harp. Jack peeped under the copper-lid and saw a most beautiful harp. The giant placed it on the table, said 'Play!' and it played of its own accord, without anybody touching it, the most exquisite music imaginable. Jack, who was a very good musician, was delighted, and more anxious to get this than any other of his enemy's treasures. But the giant not being particularly fond of music, the harp had only the effect of lulling him to sleep earlier than usual. As for the wife, she had gone to bed as soon as ever she could.

As soon as he thought all was safe, Jack got out of the copper, and, seizing the harp, was eagerly running off with it.

But the harp was enchanted by a fairy, and as soon as it found itself in strange hands it called out loudly, just as if it had been alive, 'Master! Master!'

The giant awoke, started up, and saw Jack scampering

away as fast as his legs could carry him.

'Oh, you villain! it is you who have robbed me of my hen and my money-bags, and now you are stealing my harp also. Wait till I catch you and I'll eat you up alive!'

'Very well: try!' shouted Jack, who was not a bit afraid, for he saw the giant was so tipsy he could hardly stand, much less run; and he himself had young legs and a clear conscience, which carry a man a long way. So, after leading the giant a considerable race, he contrived to be first at the top of the bean-stalk, and then scrambled down it as fast as he could, the harp playing all the while the most melancholy music till he said 'Stop,' and it stopped.

Arrived at the bottom, he found his mother sitting at her cottage door weeping silently. 'Here, mother, don't cry; just give me a hatchet—make haste.' For he knew there was not a moment to spare; he saw the giant beginning to descend the bean-stalk.

But the monster was too late—his ill deeds had come to an end. Jack with his hatchet cut the bean-stalk close off at the root. The giant fell headlong into the garden, and was killed on the spot.

Instantly the fairy appeared and explained everything to Jack's mother, begging her to forgive Jack, who was his father's own son for bravery and generosity, and who would be sure to make her happy for the rest of her days.

So all ended well, and nothing was ever more heard or seen of the wonderful bean-stalk.

10

Aladdin and the Wonderful Lamp

There once lived a poor tailor who had a son called Aladdin, a careless, idle boy who would do nothing but play all day long in the streets with little idle boys like himself. This so grieved the father that he died; yet, in spite of his mother's tears and prayers, Aladdin did not mend his ways.

One day, when he was playing in the streets as usual, a stranger asked him his age, and if he was not the son of Mustapha the tailor. 'I am, sir,' replied Aladdin; 'but he died a long while ago.' On this the stranger, who was a famous African magician, fell on his neck and kissed him, saying: 'I am your uncle, and knew you from your likeness to my brother. Go to your mother and tell her I am coming.' Aladdin ran home and told his mother of his newly found uncle. 'Indeed, child,' she said, 'your father had a brother, but I always thought he was dead.' However, she prepared supper, and bade Aladdin seek his uncle, who came laden with wine and fruit. He presently fell down and kissed the place where Mustapha used to sit, bidding Aladdin's mother not to be surprised at not having seen him before, as he had been forty years out of the country. He then turned to Aladdin, and asked him his trade, at which the boy hung his head, while his mother burst into tears. On learning that Aladdin was idle and would learn no trade, he offered to take a shop for him and stock it with merchandise. Next day he bought Aladdin a fine suit of clothes and took him all over the city, showing him the sights, and brought him home at nightfall to his mother, who was overjoyed to see her son so fine.

Next day the magician led Aladdin into some beautiful gardens a long way outside the city gates. They sat down by a fountain, and the magician pulled a cake from his girdle which he divided between them. They then journeyed onward till they almost reached the mountains. Aladdin was so tired that he begged to go back, but the magician beguiled him with pleasant stories, and led him on in spite of himself. At last they came to two mountains divided by a narrow valley.

'We will go no farther,' said the false uncle. 'I will show you something wonderful; only do you gather up sticks while I kindle a fire.' When it was lit the magician threw on it a powder he had about him, at the same time saying some magical words. The earth trembled a little and opened in front of them, disclosing a square flat stone with a brass ring in the middle to raise it by. Aladdin tried to run away, but the magician caught him and gave him a blow that knocked him down.

'What have I done, uncle?' he said, piteously; whereupon the magician said more kindly:

'Fear nothing, but obey me. Beneath this stone lies a treasure which is to be yours, and no one else may touch it, so you must do exactly as I tell you.'

At the word 'treasure' Aladdin forgot his fears, and grasped the ring as he was told, saying the names of his father and grandfather. The stone came up quite easily, and some steps appeared.

'Go down,' said the magician; 'at the foot of those steps you will find an open door leading into three large halls. Tuck up your gown and go through them without touching anything, or you will die instantly. These halls lead into a garden of fine fruit trees. Walk on till you come to a niche in a terrace where stands a lighted lamp. Pour out the oil it contains, and bring it to me.' He drew a ring from his finger and gave it to Aladdin, bidding him prosper.

Aladdin found everything as the magician had said, gathered some fruit off the trees, and, having got the lamp, arrived at the mouth of the cave. The magician cried out in a great hurry:

'Make haste and give me the lamp.' This Aladdin refused to do until he was out of the cave. The magician flew into a terrible passion, and throwing some more powder onto the fire, he said something, and the stone rolled back into its place.

The magician left Persia forever, which plainly showed that he was no uncle of Aladdin's, but a cunning magician, who had read in his magic books of a wonderful lamp, which would make him the most powerful man in the world. Though he alone knew where to find it, he could only receive it from the hand of another. He had picked out the foolish Aladdin for this purpose, intending to get the lamp and kill him afterwards.

For two days Aladdin remained in the dark, crying and lamenting. At last he clasped his hands in prayer, and in so doing rubbed the ring, which the magician had forgotten to take from him. Immediately an enormous and frightful genie rose out of the earth, saying: 'What wouldst thou with me? I am the Slave of the Ring, and will obey thee in all things.'

Aladdin fearlessly replied: 'Deliver me from this place!' whereupon the earth opened, and he found himself outside. As soon as his eyes could bear the light he went home, but fainted on the threshold. When he came to himself he told his mother what had passed, and showed her the lamp and the fruits he had gathered in the garden, which were in reality precious stones. He then asked for some food.

'Alas! child,' she said, 'I have nothing in the house, but I have spun a little cotton and will go and sell it.'

Aladdin bade her keep her cotton, for he would sell the lamp instead. As it was very dirty she began to rub it, that it might fetch a higher price. Instantly a hideous genie appeared, and asked what she would have. She fainted away, but Aladdin, snatching the lamp, said boldly: 'Fetch me something to eat!' The genie returned with a silver bowl, twelve silver plates containing rich meats, two silver cups, and two bottles of wine.

Aladdin's mother, when she came to herself, said: 'Whence comes this splendid feast?'

'Ask not, but eat,' replied Aladdin.

So they sat at breakfast till it was dinner-time, and Aladdin told his mother about the lamp. She begged him to sell it, and have nothing to do with devils. 'No,' said Aladdin, 'since chance hath made us aware of its virtues, we will use it, and the ring likewise, which I shall always wear on my finger.'

When they had eaten all the genie had brought Aladdin sold one of the silver plates, and so on until none were left. He then had recourse to the genie, who gave him another set of plates, and thus they lived for many years.

One day Aladdin heard an order from the Sultan proclaimed that every one was to stay at home and close his shutters while the Princess, his daughter, went to and from the bath. Aladdin was seized by a desire to see her face, which was very difficult, as she always went veiled. He hid himself behind the door of the bath and peeped through a chink. The Princess lifted her veil as she went in, and looked so beautiful that Aladdin fell in love with her at first sight. He went home so changed that his mother was frightened. He told her he loved the Princess so deeply that he could not live without her, and meant to ask her in marriage of her father.

His mother, on hearing this, burst out laughing, but Aladdin at last prevailed upon her to go before the Sultan and carry his request. She fetched a napkin and laid in it the magic fruits from the enchanted garden, which sparkled and shone like the most beautiful jewels. She took these with her to please the Sultan, and set out, trusting in the lamp.

The Grand Vizier and the lords of council had just gone in as she entered the hall and placed herself in front of the Sultan. He, however, took no notice of her. She went every day for a week, and stood in the same place. When the council broke up on the sixth day the Sultan said to his Vizier: 'I see a certain woman in the audience-chamber every day carrying something in a napkin. Call her next time, that I may find out what she wants.'

Next day, at a sign from the Vizier, she went up to the foot of the throne and remained kneeling till the Sultan said to her:

'Rise, good woman, and tell me what you want.' She hesitated, so the Sultan sent away all but the Vizier, and bade her speak freely, promising to forgive her beforehand for anything she might say. She then told him of her son's violent love for the Princess. 'I prayed him to forget her,' she said, 'but in vain; he threatened to do some desperate deed if I refused to go and ask your Majesty for the hand of the Princess. Now I pray you to forgive not me alone, but my son Aladdin.'

The Sultan asked her kindly what she had in the napkin, whereupon she unfolded the jewels and presented them. He was thunderstruck, and turning to the Vizier said: 'What sayest thou? Ought I not to bestow the Princess on one who values her at such a price?'

The Vizier, who wanted her for his own son, begged the Sultan to withhold her for three months, in the course of which he hoped his son would contrive to make him a richer present. The Sultan granted this, and told Aladdin's mother that, though he consented to the marriage, she must not appear before him again for three months.

Aladdin waited patiently for nearly three months, but after two had elapsed his mother, going into the city to buy oil, found every one rejoicing, and asked what was going on. 'Do you not know,' was the answer, 'that the son of the Grand Vizier is to marry the Sultan's daughter to-night?'

Breathless, she ran and told Aladdin, who was overwhelmed at first, but presently bethought him of the lamp. He rubbed it, and the genie appeared, saying: 'What is thy will?'

Aladdin replied: 'The Sultan, as thou knowest, has broken his promise to me, and the Vizier's son is to have the Princess. My command is that to-night you bring hither the bride and bridegroom.'

'Master, I obey,' said the genie.

Aladdin then went to his chamber, where, sure enough, at midnight the genie transported the bed containing the Vizier's son and the Princess.

'Take this new-married man,' he said, 'and put him outside

in the cold, and return at daybreak.' Whereupon the genie took the Vizier's son out of bed, leaving Aladdin with the Princess.

'Fear nothing,' Aladdin said to her; 'you are my wife, promised to me by your unjust father, and no harm shall come to you.'

The Princess was too frightened to speak, and passed the most miserable night of her life, while Aladdin lay down beside her and slept soundly. At the appointed hour the genie fetched in the shivering bridegroom, laid him in his place, and transported the bed back to the palace.

Presently the Sultan came to wish his daughter good-morning. The unhappy Vizier's son jumped up and hid himself, while the Princess would not say a word, and was very sorrowful. The Sultan sent her mother to her, who said: 'How comes it, child, that you will not speak to your father? What has happened?'

The Princess sighed deeply, and at last told her mother how, during the night, the bed had been carried into some strange house, and what had passed there. Her mother did not believe her in the least, but bade her rise and consider it an idle dream.

The following night exactly the same thing happened, and next morning, on the Princess's refusing to speak, the Sultan threatened to cut off her head. She then confessed all, bidding him ask the Vizier's son if it were not so. The Sultan told the Vizier to ask his son, who owned the truth, adding that, dearly as he loved the Princess, he had rather die than go through another such fearful night, and wished to be separated from her. His wish was granted, and there was an end of feasting and rejoicing.

When the three months were over, Aladdin sent his mother to remind the Sultan of his promise. She stood in the same place as before, and the Sultan, who had forgotten Aladdin, at once remembered him, and sent for her. On seeing her poverty the Sultan felt less inclined than ever to keep his word, and asked his Vizier's advice, who counselled him to set so high a value on the Princess that no man living could come up to it. The Sultan then turned to Aladdin's mother, saying: 'Good woman, a sultan must remember his promises, and I will remember mine, but your son must first send me forty basins of gold brimful of jewels, carried by forty black slaves, led by as many white ones, splendidly dressed. Tell him that I await his answer.'

The mother of Aladdin bowed low and went home, thinking all was lost. She gave Aladdin the message, adding: 'He may wait long enough for your answer!'

'Not so long, mother, as you think,' her son replied. 'I would do a great deal more than that for the Princess.' He summoned the genie, and in a few moments the eighty slaves arrived, and filled up the small house and garden. Aladdin made them set out to the palace two and two, followed by his mother. They were so richly dressed, with such splendid jewels in their girdles, that every one crowded to see them and the basins of gold they carried on their heads. They entered the palace, and, after kneeling before the Sultan, stood in a half-circle round the throne with their arms crossed, while

Aladdin's mother presented them to the Sultan.

He hesitated no longer, but said: 'Good woman, return and tell your son that I wait for him with open arms.' She lost no time in telling Aladdin, bidding him make haste.

But Aladdin first called the genie. 'I want a scented bath,' he said, 'a richly embroidered habit, a horse surpassing the Sultan's, and twenty slaves to attend me. Besides this, six slaves, beautifully dressed, to wait on my mother; and lastly, ten thousand pieces of gold in ten purses.'

No sooner said than done, Aladdin mounted his horse and passed through the streets, the slaves strewing gold as they went. Those who had played with him in his childhood knew him not, he had grown so handsome. When the Sultan saw him he came down from his throne, embraced him, and led him into a hall where a feast was spread, intending to marry him to the Princess that very day.

But Aladdin refused, saying: 'I must build a palace fit for her,' and took his leave. Once home, he said to the genie: 'Build me a palace of the finest marble, set with jasper, agate, and other precious stones. In the middle you shall build me a large hall with a dome, its four walls of massy gold and silver, each side having six windows, whose lattices, all except one which is to be unfinished, must be set with diamonds and rubies. There must be stables and horses and grooms and slaves; go and see about it!'

The palace was finished by next day, and the genie carried him there and showed him all his orders faithfully carried out, even to the laying of a velvet carpet from Aladdin's palace to the Sultan's. Aladdin's mother then dressed herself carefully, and walked to the palace with her slaves, while he followed her on horseback.

The Sultan sent musicians with trumpets and cymbals to meet them, so that the air resounded with music and cheers. She was taken to the Princess, who saluted her and treated her with great honour. At night the Princess said good-bye to her father, and set out on the carpet for Aladdin's palace, with his mother at her side, and followed by the hundred slaves. She was charmed at the sight of Aladdin, who ran to receive her. 'Princess,' he said, 'blame your beauty for my boldness if I have displeased you.' She told him that, having seen him, she willingly obeyed her father in this matter. After the wedding had taken place Aladdin led her into the hall, where a feast was spread, and she supped with him, after which they danced till midnight.

Next day Aladdin invited the Sultan to see the palace. On entering the hall with the four-and-twenty windows, with their rubies diamonds, and emeralds, he cried: 'It's a world's wonder! There is only one thing that surprises me. Was it by accident that one window was left unfinished?'

'No, sir, by design,' returned Aladdin. 'I wished your Majesty to have the glory of finishing this palace.'

The Sultan was pleased, and sent for the best jewellers in the city. He showed them the unfinished window, and bade them fit it up like the others.

'Sir,' replied their spokesman, 'we cannot find jewels enough.'

The Sultan had his own fetched, which they soon used, but to no purpose, for in a month's time the work was not half done. Aladdin, knowing that their task was vain, bade them undo their work and carry the jewels back, and the genie finished the window at his command. The Sultan was surprised to receive his jewels again, and visited Aladdin, who showed him the window finished. The Sultan embraced him, the envious Vizier meanwhile hinting that it was the work of enchantment.

Aladdin had won the hearts of the people by his gentle bearing. He was made captain of the Sultan's armies, and won several battles for him, but remained modest and courteous as before, and lived thus in peace and content for several years.

But far away in Africa the magician remembered Aladdin, and by his magic arts discovered that Aladdin, instead of perishing miserably in the cave, had escaped, and had married a princess, with whom he was living in great honour and wealth. He knew that the poor tailor's son could only have accomplished this by means of the lamp, and travelled night and day till he reached the capital of China, bent on Aladdin's ruin. As he passed through the town he heard people talking everywhere about a marvellous palace.

'Forgive my ignorance,' he asked, 'what is this palace you speak of?'

'Have you not heard of Prince Aladdin's palace,' was the reply, 'the greatest wonder of the world? I will direct you if you have a mind to see it.'

The magician thanked him who spoke, and having seen

the palace knew that it had been raised by the Genie of the Lamp, and became half mad with rage. He determined to get hold of the lamp, and again plunge Aladdin into the deepest poverty.

Unluckily, Aladdin had gone a-hunting for eight days, which gave the magician plenty of time. He bought a dozen copper lamps, put them into a basket, and went to the palace, crying: 'New lamps for old!' followed by a jeering crowd.

The Princess, sitting in the hall of four-and-twenty windows, sent a slave to find out what the noise was about, who came back laughing, so that the Princess scolded her.

'Madam,' replied the slave, 'who can help laughing to see an old fool offering to exchange fine new lamps for old ones?'

Another slave, hearing this, said, 'There is an old one on the cornice there which he can have.'

Now this was the magic lamp, which Aladdin had left there, as he could not take it out hunting with him. The Princess, not knowing its value, laughingly bade the slave take it and make the exchange.

She went and said to the magician:

'Give me a new lamp for this.'

He snatched it and bade the slave take her choice, amid the jeers of the crowd. Little he cared, but left off crying his lamps, and went out of the city gates to a lonely place, where he remained till nightfall, when he pulled out the lamp and rubbed it. The genie appeared, and at the magician's command carried him, together with the palace and the Princess in it, to a lonely place in Africa.

Next morning the Sultan looked out of the window towards Aladdin's palace and rubbed his eyes, for it was gone. He sent for the Vizier and asked what had become of the palace. The Vizier looked out, too, and was lost in astonishment. He again put it down to enchantment, and this time the Sultan believed him, and sent thirty men on horseback to fetch Aladdin in chains.

They met him riding home, bound him, and forced him to go with them on foot. The people, however, who loved him, followed, armed, to see that he came to no harm. He was carried before the Sultan, who ordered the executioner to cut off his head. The executioner made Aladdin kneel down, bandaged his eyes, and raised his scimitar to strike. At that instant the Vizier, who saw that the crowd had forced their way into the courtyard and were scaling the walls to rescue Aladdin, called to the executioner to stay his hand. The people, indeed, looked so threatening that the Sultan gave way and ordered Aladdin to be unbound, and pardoned him in the sight of the crowd. Aladdin now begged to know what he had done.

'False wretch!' said the Sultan, 'come hither,' and showed him from the window the place where his palace had stood.

Aladdin was so amazed that he could not say a word. 'Where is my palace and my daughter?' demanded the Sultan. 'For the first I am not so deeply concerned, but my daughter I must have, and you must find her or lose your head.'

Aladdin begged for forty days in which to find her, promising if he failed to return and suffer death at the Sultan's pleasure. His prayer was granted, and he went forth sadly from the Sultan's presence.

For three days he wandered about like a madman, asking every one what had become of his palace, but they only laughed and pitied him. He came to the banks of a river, and knelt down to say his prayers before throwing himself in. In so doing he rubbed the magic ring he still wore. The genie he had seen in the cave appeared, and asked his will.

'Save my life, genie,' said Aladdin, 'and bring my palace back.'

'That is not in my power,' said the genie; 'I am only the Slave of the Ring; you must ask him of the lamp.'

'Even so,' said Aladdin, 'but thou canst take me to the palace, and set me down under my dear wife's window.' He at once found himself in Africa, under the window of the Princess, and fell asleep out of sheer weariness.

He was awakened by the singing of the birds, and his heart was lighter. He saw plainly that all his misfortunes were owing to the loss of the lamp, and vainly wondered who had robbed him of it.

That morning the Princess rose earlier than she had done since she had been carried into Africa by the magician, whose company she was forced to endure once a day. She, however, treated him so harshly that he dared not live there altogether. As she was dressing, one of her women looked out and saw

Aladdin. The Princess ran and opened the window, and at the noise she made Aladdin looked up. She called to him to come to her, and great was the joy of these lovers at seeing each other again.

After he had kissed her, Aladdin said: 'I beg of you, Princess, in God's name, before we speak of anything else, for your own sake and mine, tell me what has become of an old lamp I left on the cornice in the hall of four-and-twenty windows, when I went a-hunting.'

'Alas!' she said, 'I am the innocent cause of our sorrows,' and told him of the exchange of the lamp.

'Now I know,' cried Aladdin, 'that we have to thank the African magician for this! Where is the lamp?'

'He carries it about with him,' said the Princess. 'I know, for he pulled it out of his breast to show me. He wishes me to break my faith with you and marry him, saying that you were beheaded by my father's command. He is forever speaking ill of you, but I only reply by my tears. If I persist, I doubt not but he will use violence.'

Aladdin comforted her, and left her for a while. He changed clothes with the first person he met in the town, and having bought a certain powder returned to the Princess, who let him in by a little side door. 'Put on your most beautiful dress,' he said to her, 'and receive the magician with smiles, leading him to believe that you have forgotten me. Invite him to supper with you, and say you wish to taste the wine of his country. He will go for some and while he is gone I will tell you what to do.'

She listened carefully to Aladdin, and when he left her arrayed herself gayly for the first time since she left China.

She put on a girdle and head-dress of diamonds, and seeing in a glass that she was more beautiful than ever, received the magician, saying, to his great amazement: 'I have made up my mind that Aladdin is dead, and that all my tears will not bring him back to me, so I am resolved to mourn no more, and have therefore invited you to sup with me; but I am tired of the wines of China, and would fain taste those of Africa.'

The magician flew to his cellar, and the Princess put the powder Aladdin had given her in her cup. When he returned she asked him to drink her health in the wine of Africa, handing him her cup in exchange for his, as a sign she was reconciled to him.

Before drinking the magician made her a speech in praise of her beauty, but the Princess cut him short, saying: 'Let us drink first, and you shall say what you will afterwards.'

She set her cup to her lips and kept it there, while the magician drained his to the dregs and fell back lifeless. The Princess then opened the door to Aladdin, and flung her arms round his neck; but Aladdin put her away, bidding her leave him, as he had more to do. He then went to the dead magician, took the lamp out of his vest, and bade the genie carry the palace and all in it back to China. This was done, and the Princess in her chamber only felt two little shocks, and little thought she was at home again.

The Sultan, who was sitting in his closet, mourning for his lost daughter, happened to look up, and rubbed his eyes, for there stood the palace as before. He hastened thither, and Aladdin received him in the hall of the four-and-twenty windows, with the Princess at his side.

Aladdin told him what had happened, and showed him the dead body of the magician, that he might believe. A ten days' feast was proclaimed, and it seemed as if Aladdin might now live the rest of his life in peace; but it was not to be.

The African magician had a younger brother, who was, if possible, more wicked and more cunning than himself. He travelled to China to avenge his brother's death, and went to visit a pious woman called Fatima, thinking she might be of use to him. He entered her cell and clapped a dagger to her breast, telling her to rise and do his bidding on pain of death. He changed clothes with her, coloured his face like hers, put on her veil, and murdered her, that she might tell no tales. Then he went towards the palace of Aladdin, and all the people, thinking he was the holy woman, gathered round him, kissing his hands and begging his blessing.

When he got to the palace there was such a noise going on round him that the Princess bade her slave look out of the window and ask what was the matter. The slave said it was the holy woman, curing people by her touch of their ailments, whereupon the Princess, who had long desired to see Fatima, sent for her. On coming to the Princess the magician offered up a prayer for her health and prosperity. When he had done the Princess made him sit by her, and begged him to stay with her always. The false Fatima, who wished for nothing better, consented, but kept his veil down for fear of discovery. The Princess showed him the hall, and asked him what he thought of it.

'It is truly beautiful,' said the false Fatima. 'In my mind it wants but one thing.'

'And what is that?' said the Princess.

'If only a roc's egg,' replied he, 'were hung up from the middle of this dome, it would be the wonder of the world.'

After this the Princess could think of nothing but the roc's egg, and when Aladdin returned from hunting he found her in a very ill humour. He begged to know what was amiss, and she told him that all her pleasure in the hall was spoiled for the want of a roc's egg hanging from the dome. 'If that is all,' replied Aladdin, 'you shall soon be happy.' He left her and rubbed the lamp, and when the genie appeared commanded him to bring a roc's egg.

The genie gave such a loud and terrible shriek that the hall shook. 'Wretch!' he cried, 'is it not enough that I have done everything for you but you must command me to bring my master and hang him up in the midst of this dome? You and your wife and your palace deserve to be burnt to ashes but that this request does not come from you, but from the brother of the African magician whom you destroyed. He is now in your palace disguised as the holy woman—whom he murdered. He it was who put that wish into your wife's head. Take care of yourself, for he means to kill you.' So saying, the genie disappeared.

Aladdin went back to the Princess, saying his head ached, and requesting that the holy Fatima should be fetched to lay her hands on it. But when the magician came near, Aladdin, seizing his dagger, pierced him to the heart.

'What have you done?' cried the Princess. 'You have killed the holy woman!'

'Not so,' replied Aladdin, 'but a wicked magician,' and told her of how she had been deceived.

After this Aladdin and his wife lived in peace. He succeeded the Sultan when he died, and reigned for many years, leaving behind him a long line of kings.

Acknowledgements

This completed work is a synergistic product of many minds.

I thank my husband, Rishi Sehgal, my entire family and all my dear friends for being patient and encouraging.

I bear a deep sense of sincere appreciation for Yamini Chowdhury for her efficient and professional approach to the work. My earnest regards to Aditi Mehrotra for devoting her valuable time and giving editorial inputs, which has helped shape this book. I express my gratitude to the most diligent team of Rupa Publications for their efforts.

To acknowledge is to express my gratitude to all of you who undoubtedly remain an integral part of my extraordinary journey. Your unwavering support and encouragement have truly made this book possible.